Welcome to the Secret World of Alex Mack!

I've always liked Halloween, but this year was something else! For years I've gone trick-or-treating in the same costume—and liked it! But my friends Nicole and Robyn hate it. So this year I promised I'd be a space alien with them, complete with green makeup and purple hair. Then reports of alien sightings set off a major panic in town. That's when things got a bit out of hand, even for Halloween! Let me explain. . . .

I'm Alex Mack. I was just another average kid until my first day of junior high.

One minute I'm walking home from school—the next there's a *crash!* A truck from the Paradise Valley Chemical plant overturns in front of me, and I'm drenched in some weird chemical.

And since then—well, nothing's been the same. I can move objects with my mind, shoot electrical charges through my fingertips, and morph into a liquid shape . . . which is handy when I get in a tight spot!

My best friend, Ray, thinks it's cool—and my sister, Annie, thinks I'm a science project.

They're the only two people who know about my new powers. I can't let anyone else find out—not even my parents—because I know the chemical plant wants to find me and turn me into some experiment.

But you know something? I guess I'm not so average anymore!

The Secret World of Alex Mack™

Available from MINSTREL Books

Halloween Invaders!

John Vornholt

St. Louis de Montfort Catholic School
Fishers, IN

A
MINSTREL®
BOOK

Published by POCKET BOOKS
New York   London   Toronto   Sydney   Tokyo   Singapore

This book is a work of fiction. Names, characters, places and
incidents are products of the author's imagination or are used
fictitiously. Any resemblance to actual events or locales or persons, living or dead, is entirely coincidental.

A MINSTREL PAPERBACK *Original*

A Minstrel Book published by
POCKET BOOKS, a division of Simon & Schuster Inc.
1230 Avenue of the Americas, New York, NY 10020

Copyright © 1997 by Viacom International Inc., and RHI Enter-
tainment Inc. All rights reserved. Based on the Nickelodeon
series entitled "The Secret World of Alex Mack."

ISBN: 0-671-00708-4

First Minstrel Books printing October 1997

10 9 8 7 6 5 4 3 2 1

Cover photography by Thomas Queally and Danny Feld

Printed in the U.S.A.

For Sarah and Eric

Halloween Invaders!

CHAPTER 1

"You can't do it, Alex. You just can't do it!" Nicole Wilson twisted her face into a look of horror.

"That's right," Robyn Russo agreed. "If you do that again, your reputation will be finished."

"I won't be seen with you," Nicole warned. "It would be too horrible, even for me."

Alex Mack frowned at her so-called friends, who sat side by side on her bed. "It's *my* life, you know."

"And you're *ruining* it," Robyn said with a groan. "People will be talking about you behind your back."

Nicole nodded in agreement. "I don't think

anybody in Paradise Valley can stand to see it again. I know *I* can't.''

Alex pointed at the red-and-white-checked costume hanging on the closet door of her bedroom. ''Okay, give me one good reason why I shouldn't go out on Halloween dressed as Raggedy Ann.''

Robyn crossed her arms and looked sternly at Alex. ''How about the fact that you always go out on Halloween dressed as Raggedy Ann?''

''Well, it's good to have consistency in life,'' Alex replied. ''That way people don't have to guess who I am.''

''If people know who you are on Halloween, you've missed the whole point,'' Nicole said, rolling her eyes. ''Halloween is about being somebody else, being mysterious, being *weird*.''

Alex had never told her girlfriends how weird she really was since getting doused with GC-161, a chemical with some very potent properties. If she wanted a strange costume, all she had to do was morph into a liquid silvery blob. That was only one of the amazing powers Alex had acquired from the GC-161 that might be weird enough even for Nicole.

But she couldn't tell her friends about her superpowers because she had to protect them.

Ruthless people from the Paradise Valley Chemical Plant were determined to find the GC-161 kid, and she didn't want to get her friends involved. Her parents didn't even know what had happened to Alex. It was bad enough that her sister, Annie, and Ray Alvarado knew about her plight and could be endangered.

"Besides," said Robyn, "that costume is falling apart. I bet it doesn't even fit you anymore."

Alex touched the hem of the checked dress and noticed that it *was* frayed. Last year, the dress had been a little tight, and she had grown since then. Of course, these were all things that could be fixed.

"And that wig!" Robyn said with disgust. "It looks like something that got run over on the highway."

"Okay, okay," said Alex. "I'd go without a costume, but that's what Annie does. I don't want to copy her, because I think that's totally boring. We've only got a couple of days till Halloween, so what should I wear?"

"Now we're talking," said Robyn, clapping her hands together. "Science fiction is hot this year, so why don't you go as an alien from outer space? That's what Nicole and I are doing."

Alex frowned. "I don't want to wear a big, heavy mask or a gross costume."

"No way," said Robyn. "We'll go as *attractive* aliens, not ugly ones. It'll be like a retro-futuristic thing. We'll get some miniskirts, sparkly tops, weird-colored tights, and rubber ears. We can wear green face makeup and purple hair tint. We'll look good."

"Isn't that what Nicole usually wears every day?" Alex joked.

"Funny." Nicole got a faraway look in her eyes. "You know, I believe there are aliens out there. I'm positive they walk among us. Some of them probably live right here in Paradise Valley."

"Oh, they can't be *that* boring," said Robyn. "If you could go anywhere in the universe, would you hang out in Paradise Valley? I don't think so."

"Well," said Alex thoughtfully, "weird things do happen here every now and then."

"I hope those aliens don't watch our movies," said Nicole with concern. "They always get treated like the bad guys in movies. I think we should be friendly to them, not scared. After all, they wouldn't come here unless they wanted to help us."

4

"Or *eat* us," Alex said with a spooky laugh.

Frowning, Nicole looked at her watch. "I've got to go to the dentist, but we need to shop for our costumes. See you later at the mall?"

"Yeah, the mall!" Robyn answered with a grin.

Alex sighed. "Do we have to go there?"

Robyn shook her head in amazement. "You must be the only teenager in America who doesn't like to go to the mall."

"Listen," said Alex, "we could go to that really creepy thrift shop downtown and save ourselves some money. They probably have the same stuff, only cheaper."

Nicole huffed and said, "Alex, you're too practical. But okay, the thrift shop it is. See you later."

A few minutes later, Alex and Robyn were walking along the sidewalk, headed downtown. There was a chill in the air and it was definitely autumn. Golden-red leaves sailed through the air like a fleet of kites, and the smells of cinnamon and apple pies wafted on the breeze.

Robyn was still planning their costumes, wondering whether they should be green-skinned or blue-skinned aliens. Which would look better with her blue eyes?

"Hey, Mack! Wait up!" a voice called. Alex and Robyn turned around to see Ray and Louis Driscoll running to catch up with them.

What a funny pair they are, Alex thought. Ray was tall and gangly and he was a real nice guy. He had been her best friend for as long as she could remember. Louis was short and red-haired, and had a very high opinion of himself. He wanted everybody to think he was funny and handsome, when he was really a bit insecure.

"Where are you guys going?" asked Ray.

"We've got to shop for our Halloween costumes," Robyn said.

Ray gripped his chest, looking shocked. "You mean Alex isn't going to go as Raggedy Ann?"

"No," said Robyn, "we're going as aliens from outerspace. Cute ones, with purple hair and miniskirts."

"Be still, my heart." Louis grinned at Alex.

"Don't make a big deal out of it," Alex warned, "or I'll fix up my old costume."

"No! No!" everyone cried at once.

"We won't say another word," Ray promised, falling into step with the girls.

Louis's eyes twinkled with mischief. "Wait until you hear what I have planned for Halloween. And all of you can help me."

Alex rolled her eyes. "Forget it. We're not going to scare off the little kids trick-or-treating so you can get all the best candy."

"No, not that again," said Louis. "I've grown beyond candy. I'm going to deejay at the school radio station on Halloween night!"

"Cool!" said Robyn. "What music are you going to play?"

"The usual stuff, 'Monster Mash' and 'The Chipmunks Sing the Theme from *Psycho.*'" Louis looked around and lowered his voice. "But it's not the music I'm going to play that's important—it's the *trick* I'm going to play."

Alex frowned. She knew that when Louis decided to be funny, everybody had better look out. "What exactly are you going to do?"

"I've been reading about Orson Welles and the *War of the Worlds* radio scare he pulled on Halloween in 1938. He put on a version of H. G. Wells's *War of the Worlds* in the form of a newscast. It convinced the whole country that Martians had actually invaded earth. It caused a panic!"

Louis grinned. "I'm going to do something like that. I'll have a call-in show, and all of my friends will call me. But some of you guys will claim you've seen UFOs landing, and aliens running around. It'll be a scream!"

"Cool!" said Robyn. "Count me in."

Alex nodded, impressed. This was better than most of Louis's ideas. "Okay," she said. "I'll call in, too. It might be fun."

Ray clapped his hands. "If Alex says it's a good idea, it's gotta be great. Come on, let's go tell more people!"

"Wait a minute, guys," said Robyn. "Do me a favor and don't tell Nicole. She thinks all that stuff about extraterrestrials is true. You could really trick her in a big way." The usually pessimistic Robyn had a mischievous glint in her eye that lit up her face.

"She's right," said Louis. "We'll be careful how many people we tell. Catch you later."

As the two boys rushed off, Robyn looked at Alex and grinned. "This might be the best Halloween ever!"

"I don't know," Alex said sadly. This time she was feeling like the pessimist. "It won't be the same without Raggedy Ann."

It was dark by the time the three girls finished their shopping and headed for home. Alex called her house to make sure that she wouldn't be late for dinner, but nobody was home. Her dad had a heavy-duty project going at the chemical plant, and both her mom and her sister had full class loads, so they sometimes postponed dinner.

As Alex, Robyn, and Nicole continued walking, they saw a really bright flash of light streak across the sky.

"Wow, did you see that?" Nicole gushed. "A shooting star! Make a wish."

"That looked brighter than a shooting star," Alex said with a frown. "I wonder what it was. It even looked too bright to be a meteorite."

"Maybe some of that space junk," said Robyn. "You could be lying at home in bed, and some old satellite could crash through the roof and kill you."

"You always look on the bright side," said Alex.

"Well, it's true," Robyn protested.

They reached the intersection. Alex's street was down one way, and Robyn and Nicole had to go the other way. Robyn was carrying the bags with their makeup, costumes, and hair tint. "Do you want me to hold on to this stuff?" she asked.

"Sure," said Alex. "I doubt if I'll want to wear

any green makeup or antennas until Halloween. It's only the day after tomorrow."

"I'll probably get dressed at home and meet you," said Nicole. She took her things out of the bags and put them in her backpack.

"Hey, Nicole," said Robyn, "Louis is going to be the Halloween deejay on the school radio station. Make sure you listen." She gave Alex a wink.

After saying good night, Alex walked slowly home, enjoying the cool autumn evening. She could smell logs burning in fireplaces up and down the street, and she could hear a football game on somebody's car radio. On a night like this, Paradise Valley seemed like the most peaceful place on earth.

When she got to her house Alex saw that nobody was home. She unlocked the door and went into the kitchen, where she found a note from her dad. Her parents and Annie were at a dinner honoring Danielle Atron, the CEO of the chemical plant. *Well, that's one event I don't mind missing,* Alex thought.

There was leftover tuna casserole for dinner, which Alex liked. She fixed herself a bowl and put it in the microwave oven to heat. While she ate, she leafed through a bunch of catalogs that had come in the mail. Advertisers seemed to want Christmas shoppers to start around Halloween.

As she was washing the dishes, the doorbell rang. Alex looked at the clock over the oven and saw that it was 8:30. Who would be coming by the house this time of night?

She went to the front door and peered through the peephole. Standing outside was a tall, older man wearing a dark suit and tie and carrying a suitcase and a newspaper in his hands. He looked too distinguished to be a salesman.

Alex wondered if this stranger was connected with the chemical plant. Was he looking for the GC-161 kid? Vince had been fired, but that didn't mean the PVC people had stopped looking for her. It only meant that people she didn't know were now doing the looking.

But the man looked very patient as he stood on her front doorstep. He was mysterious, but not threatening. She decided to open the door and see what he wanted, although she would keep the chain on. "Can I help you?" she asked.

He smiled briefly and held up the newspaper. "I hope so. My name is Mr. Jonathan Smith, and I saw in the classified ads that you have a room to rent."

Alex frowned. "Can I see that?" she asked.

He handed her the newspaper, and she looked at the want ad. It only took her a moment to figure out what was wrong. "I think this is a misprint. The first two numbers are probably 'thirty-two,' not 'twenty-three.' The house you want is across the street. That blue one."

"Are you sure?" asked Mr. Smith. He looked a little confused, as if house numbers were new to him.

"Yes. In fact, I remember that Mrs. Brownstein said she was going to rent out a room. That's the one you want." She smiled. "I'm Alex Mack. Maybe you'll be our neighbor."

"That would be nice," Mr. Smith said pleasantly. "Thank you for your help, Miss Mack." He started off.

"Will you be staying a long time?" asked Alex.

The tall man stopped and looked back at her. "I'm not sure yet. I have some . . . research to do."

"I see," said Alex. "Well, good luck."

"Thank you." The man walked away, and Alex thought that he was the most polite man she had ever met.

Almost too polite.

CHAPTER 2

The next morning, on her way to school, Alex saw Mr. Jonathan Smith leave Mrs. Brownstein's house. Once again, he was wearing a dark suit and tie. He looked as if he had learned to dress by watching old movies. He was walking her way, so she couldn't avoid him.

"Hello, Miss Mack," he said pleasantly.

"Hello, Mr. Smith," she answered. "I guess you're our new neighbor."

"Yes, I am. I'm sorry for any problems I caused last night."

"Oh, no problem," she answered. "I'm glad you found the right house."

"Thanks to you." He smiled. "Could I ask for some more advice from you?"

Alex shrugged. "Sure."

"I'm looking for the Paradise Valley Chemical Plant. Perhaps you could tell me where it is?"

He sure must be a stranger, Alex thought. Half the people in town either worked for the plant or provided some service to them. Everyone knew where it was. Alex was suddenly wary. Why did Mr. Smith want to go to the chemical plant?

"The plant is out on the interstate," said Alex. "But that's miles away. You can't walk there."

"I assure you," said Mr. Smith, "I can walk many miles without tiring."

"But you don't have to," said Alex. "My dad works there, and he can give you a ride. Come on, I'll introduce you." She took Mr. Smith through the back door into the kitchen, where Annie and her dad were still finishing breakfast.

"Dad, Annie, this is Mr. Smith," said Alex. "He took the spare room in Mrs. Brownstein's house, so he's our new neighbor."

"Hello," said Annie. She flashed Alex a look, which meant that she wanted to learn more about him later.

"Pleased to meet you," said her dad. "I'm George Mack. My wife, Barbara, had to leave early for school, but you can meet her some other time. Would you like some coffee?"

"No, thank you," said Mr. Smith. "Alex tells me that you work at the Paradise Valley Chemical Plant."

"That's right." George took a drink of orange juice.

The stranger smiled. "I'd like to go there and find out more about GC-161."

Somehow, Alex managed not to gasp, choke, or cry out from the shock of hearing what the man's mission was. But her eyes locked with Annie's, and she could see her sister was also making a humongous effort to stay cool.

George spit out a mouthful of orange juice. He quickly wiped his chin with his napkin. "Excuse me, but GC-161 is supposed to be a secret," he sputtered.

"Is it?" asked Mr. Smith pleasantly. "I've known about GC-161 for a long time."

"How?" George asked in amazement.

Mr. Smith narrowed his eyes. "I'm afraid I can't tell you that."

"Where are you from?" Annie asked suspiciously.

"Far away," Mr. Smith answered. Alex believed him. There was definitely something very strange about Mr. Smith.

"Could you take me to the plant?" asked the stranger.

"I could, but nobody will tell you anything about the chemical," said George.

"I have to try," Mr. Smith answered.

Alex began to sneak toward the door. "Excuse me, I've got to go, or I'm going to be late for school. Bye, everybody!"

She tried to run, but Annie caught up with her in the driveway.

"What's going on?" asked Annie. "Who is this guy?"

Alex shrugged. "He came to our house last night because he got the addresses mixed up. I think he's just a neighbor who lives across the street from us. I hope so, anyway."

Annie whispered, "He's more than just a neighbor. Nobody outside the plant knows about GC-161. How does *he* know?"

"Beats me," Alex answered. "You can bet *I* didn't tell him."

Annie frowned. "No, I guess you wouldn't do that. Well, we have to keep an eye on him. I hope he doesn't get us into trouble. He dresses like he's out of some old movie."

"I know. Listen, gotta run." Alex moved off down the driveway, asking over her shoulder, "What are you going to do for Halloween?"

"Hand out candy, as usual," Annie answered.

"No date this year?"

"No date. I've learned my lesson."

Alex walked briskly to school, still thinking about the mysterious Mr. Smith. He had shown up about an hour after she saw that weird meteorite, which was much brighter than a normal meteorite. He wouldn't say where he was from, except that it was "far away." And he knew about stuff he shouldn't know about.

Could he maybe, possibly, be from outer space? Alex wondered.

No, she thought with a laugh. She had been listening to Nicole too much, and thinking too much about her costume. Sure, there would be aliens out in droves on Halloween, but they would just be kids in costumes. Some of them would be on the radio, in Louis's silly stunt.

But none of them would be real. . . .

It was an exciting day at school, with Halloween being only one day away. Everyone was talking about their costumes and how much fun that night would be. There would also be a dance and a couple of parties to go to.

All day long Alex couldn't stop thinking about Mr. Smith. He seemed sort of sad and lonely, as if he really was a long way from home. And he acted as if GC-161 was something you just talked about, like the weather.

More than anybody on earth, Alex knew how powerful the chemical was. But she had a strange feeling that Mr. Smith also knew how potent it was. What else did he want to know? At least he didn't appear to be interested in finding the "GC-161 kid."

After the final bell, Alex stopped by her locker to pick up her jacket and backpack. Everybody she knew came by to tell her something.

"Remember," said Robyn, "right after school tomorrow, come over to my house. We'll start getting dressed."

"It's going to take us three hours to get dressed?" Alex asked doubtfully.

"At least," Robyn answered. "Don't forget. We have to tint our hair and put on makeup. It'll be fun!" She hurried off.

Ray was the next one to stop by her locker. "You know," he said, "I'm really looking forward to seeing you in some other costume besides Raggedy Ann. The last time you wore another costume, I think we were ten years old. You were a fairy princess."

"Please," said Alex, "I was never a fairy princess. Well, maybe when I was four years old."

"That's right," Ray agreed. "I've known you a long time, haven't I?"

"Yeah," said Alex wistfully.

"Then can I still have all your candy bars with coconut in them?"

Alex laughed. She didn't like coconut. "Okay. I always save them for you, anyway."

Then Louis sidled up to them. He took off his sunglasses and lowered his voice. "Remember, Mack, you've got to listen to my show tomorrow night. Ray will call in first and give us the first report. After that, it's to you and Robyn." He winked. "Make the story good. You know, like you saw a weird light in the sky, then this spaceman came to your door."

Alex gulped, trying not to think about Mr. Smith. "Okay," she said. "Weird lights, spacemen—I can do that."

"You sure can," Ray said with a knowing smile.

Louis put his sunglasses back on. "Come on,

Ray. You've got to help me pick out some tunes to play tomorrow."

"Yeah," said Ray, "you can't play all that hokey stuff with the Chipmunks."

"How about *Elvira's Greatest Hits?*" Louis asked as they walked away.

Alex sighed. She almost wished that Halloween was over. It was hardly her favorite holiday, maybe because her whole life was too much like Halloween. She grabbed her jacket and backpack and hurried out the front door of the high school.

As Alex reached her house, she heard a door open and shut across the street. For some reason, she stopped and turned around.

There was Mr. Smith standing on the sidewalk, looking at her with his intense gray eyes. "Miss Mack," he said, "may I please speak with you?"

Alex took a deep breath and thought about telling him no. But he looked so somber, even sad. There was nobody home at her house, so she didn't want to invite him in.

"Let me get rid of my backpack," she said, "and we'll go for a walk."

"Thank you, Miss Mack."

She left him standing on the sidewalk as she

ducked into her house to hang up her backpack. When she returned, Mr. Smith was standing exactly where she had left him. He had barely moved a muscle. His suit still looked as if it had been freshly pressed.

"Thank you for talking to me, Miss Mack," he began.

"Can I ask a favor of you?"

"Certainly."

"Would you please call me 'Alex'? Nobody calls me 'Miss Mack.' "

He smiled. "As you wish. Do I act too formal?"

"Yes, you sure do. Where are you from, anyway?"

"That isn't important." Mr. Smith began to walk down the sidewalk, and Alex fell into step beside him.

"How did you do at the chemical plant?" she asked.

He frowned. "Not very well. I asked to see Ms. Atron and they threw me out. In fact, they threatened to call the police."

"Yes, that's our lovely Ms. Atron," said Alex. "And my dad didn't tell you anything, did he?"

"No, but I respect his position. Still, I'm worried about this GC-161. I'm afraid the people at the plant don't know how powerful that chemical compound is. It's very unstable."

"I wouldn't know anything about it," said Alex cautiously. Her heart beat a little faster, though.

Mr. Smith smiled at her. "You seem to be a very intelligent young woman."

"No," said Alex, "that's my sister. She got all the brains and I got all the bad luck."

The stranger lowered his voice. "If that's the case, then why did they experiment on *you* with the GC-161?"

Alex stopped dead in her tracks and stared at the man. Then she tried to laugh it off. "I . . . I don't know what you're talking about."

"I see," Mr. Smith said thoughtfully. "Is it possible they don't know about you? Did your father perform the experiment?"

"He doesn't know anything about it!" she blurted out. Alex bit her lip. "Now I've got a question. Do you really work for the plant?"

He laughed, and it was a rich, pleasant sound. "No, as I told you, they threw me out, didn't even want to talk to me. How do I know about you? Let's just say we have instruments that are more powerful than theirs. It was no accident that I came to this neighborhood."

"Who's 'we'?" asked Alex.

The man shrugged. "You aren't being entirely honest with me, Alex, so I see no reason to be entirely honest with you. Perhaps it's better that we hold on to our little secrets."

"Yeah," said Alex thoughtfully. She wanted to ask the man if he could help her get rid of the effects of the GC-161. But then she would have to admit to what he was saying.

"Don't worry," said Mr. Smith. "I won't tell anyone about you. In fact, my mission is over. I'll leave here tomorrow, and you'll never see me again."

Alex stared down at the ground. "Suppose a person did get covered with this GC-161 stuff—could they have a normal life?"

"Your life probably wouldn't be 'normal,' " Mr. Smith said. "You would be a very special human being. However, the compound usually isn't fatal."

"Good," Alex said with a sigh. "I mean, good for somebody that might happen to."

"I think so," said Mr. Smith. "Good-bye, Alex. It's been a pleasure knowing you."

He started walking off, and Alex called after him, "Mr. Smith!"

"Yes?"

"You might want to stick around tomorrow night."

"Really. Why?"

Alex smiled. "It's Halloween, and that's usually a big deal in Paradise Valley. I wouldn't go out if I were you, but I'd watch it from my window."

Mr. Smith nodded thoughtfully. "Halloween. Yes, that sounds interesting. Thank you, Alex, I'll stay to see it. Good-bye."

"Good-bye, Mr. Smith."

Alex hoped she would never see the mysterious stranger again. But in an odd way, she would miss him.

CHAPTER 3

On Halloween night, there were lit pumpkins on every doorstep. The sidewalks were full of little goblins, ghosts, skeletons, and even some fairy princesses. They carried bags and buckets full of candy, and their proud parents walked along with them, holding flashlights.

Also roaming the streets were bigger kids, and they wore horrible rubber masks and vampire makeup. They had bigger bags full of candy, because they hit more houses than the little kids. Plenty of adults were dressed in costume, too, as they strolled through town on their way to Halloween parties.

Alex sat by the window of Robyn's bedroom,

watching the scene on the street below. Her scalp itched, because Robyn had coated her hair with purple tint. She was beginning to wish that she had simply brought her old Raggedy Ann wig—after all, there was no rule that aliens had to have nice hair.

But, no, Robyn was going all out. Alex had to admit that the striped tights, shiny miniskirts, and sparkling tops looked pretty cool. But she wasn't so sure about the green makeup, glitter, rubber ears, and antennas. That stuff made Robyn look more like a giant ladybug than an alien.

"Hold still," said Robyn. She dipped her fingers into a jar of green greasepaint and spread a big gob of it on Alex's forehead. Alex tried to hold still, but she had never liked makeup much, especially not bright green makeup.

"I'm going to look like Kermit the Frog," she complained.

"Now, does Kermit have purple hair?" asked Robyn.

"No. I guess that makes him smarter than me," Alex answered.

"If you don't stop complaining," said Robyn, "I'm going to leave you half human and half alien."

No big deal, thought Alex. *I feel like that most of the time, anyway.* But she said nothing. Next year she would make her own costume—a brand-new Raggedy Ann dress that fit her perfectly. And she would wear it until she got too old to go out on Halloween.

At least Louis was playing cool music on his radio show. That was mostly thanks to Ray, of course. Louis wouldn't know cool music if someone dropped a stack of CDs on his head.

They listened to the voice of Vincent Price, with his trademark evil laugh, at the end of a selection. Then Louis broke in: "That was 'Thriller' by Michael Jackson. This is your dee-jay, Louis Driscoll, on KPVH, Paradise High School. Hope you're having a howling Halloween! Don't forget, listeners, this is a request show. Feel free to call in and make your request. But no Chipmunks, please. Our number is 555-4388."

"I'm almost done," said Robyn as she applied green gunk to Alex's neck. Alex's stomach began to feel a bit queasy, and she hoped she hadn't eaten too much of Robyn's family's candy already. The night was still young.

Just then a ringing noise came over the air.

Louis didn't sound very surprised when he said, "Oh, there's a call now."

Robyn stopped putting makeup on Alex and waited. She grinned at Alex, who tried to smile back. But her stomach was feeling very strange.

"Hello, caller, what do you want to hear?" asked Louis.

"No, this isn't about music—this is an emergency!" the caller shouted.

Robyn howled with laughter, because the caller was clearly Ray, trying to disguise his voice.

"What's the matter?" Louis asked, sounding concerned.

"I saw a UFO out at the old quarry! There was a flash of light, and this huge, glowing mother ship landed. I heard a bunch of eerie noises, then the spaceship began to morph. It burped out these weird aliens. That's when I took off running!"

"Oh, come on, it's Halloween," said Louis. He was putting on a pretty good act.

"No, I'm serious," said Ray. "The aliens went off in different directions, like they were heading all over town. If you look outside, you'll see them!"

"What a perfect time to invade earth," said

Louis, sounding serious. "Who would know they were aliens on Halloween?"

With a big grin on her face, Robyn leaned across her bed to get the telephone. "It's our turn next," she said to Alex.

Alex frowned and the thick makeup on her face cracked like dried mud. "I'm not so sure we should do this. I mean, it's not nice to make fun of alien beings."

"Oh, come on," Robyn scoffed. "Now you sound like Nicole. You don't believe there are such things, do you?" She punched the number on her telephone, winking conspiratorially at Alex.

"We have another call," Louis said importantly. "Hang on, please." There was a click, and he answered, "This is KPVH. Do you have a request?"

"No!" Robyn said breathlessly. "I saw them, too—the aliens. They came down my street, and they . . . they tried to grab some kids, but they got away. This is no joke! The aliens are out there, and they're real!" She covered her mouth to keep from laughing.

"Oh, no!" said Louis, sounding worried. "Could this really be happening? What did they look like?"

Robyn looked at Alex's hair for inspiration. "Well, they were sort of shiny and wavy—all purple and blue. They definitely were not human, and not people in costumes, either!"

"Thank you, caller," said Louis. "We had better free up these phone lines, in case there are any more reports."

"Heaven help us!" Robyn said in a panicky voice. She hung up the phone and burst out laughing.

Then she handed the phone to Alex. "It's your turn."

Alex took a deep breath. She wasn't feeling very well, and she didn't think the joke was very funny anymore.

"Come on," said Robyn, "you promised you'd do it."

"Okay." Alex didn't want to be a spoilsport. She dialed the number and waited for Louis to answer.

"Alien hotline," he said importantly.

"I saw them, too," Alex said in a deep voice. "Only I don't think they mean us any harm. Maybe they're friendly."

"But how do we know that?" asked Louis. "What if they're doing what aliens always do—you know, grab people and perform weird experiments on them. What a perfect night to do it, when so many people are out on the streets!"

The phone kept ringing. "Hold on, I have another call."

There was a click on the phone as Alex was put on hold. Over the radio came a strange voice, the voice of an older man: "I didn't see the UFO tonight, but I sure saw a UFO two nights ago. It streaked right over town—I think it landed in a cornfield."

Puzzled, Robyn looked at Alex. "Who is *that?* It doesn't sound like anybody we know." Alex shrugged.

"Is that right?" said Louis, sounding surprised as well. "Our switchboard is lighting up. The calls are pouring in! We don't want anyone to panic, but it does seem as if aliens have invaded Paradise Valley on Halloween!"

Alex hung up the phone. Her stomach was churning. She was sure she'd be turning green, if she wasn't already.

Within the next few minutes, there were more calls. Some were friends of Louis's, but others were adults who said they had seen the UFO two nights earlier. Alex wondered if she should go warn Mr. Smith, but she didn't feel well enough even to walk home.

"Can you believe that?" asked Robyn. "Other people are horning in on *our* Halloween trick. We might as well listen to another station." She tuned the radio to a regular rock station.

A commercial was just ending, when a female deejay broke in. "I don't want to alarm anyone," she said, "but we're hearing reports of UFOs tonight. And there have even been reports of space aliens on the streets of Paradise Valley.

"Not only that," she went on, "but there were reports of a UFO two nights ago. I know a lot of people saw the spaceship. We have operators standing by, so if you see UFOs or space aliens, give us a call."

Robyn grinned. "What do you know, Louis hit the big time! Hey—do you think that was a UFO we saw two nights ago? You know, when we saw that bright light flash across the sky?"

"I thought you didn't believe in those things," said Alex.

"Well, you never know."

The phone rang, and Robyn answered it. "Hi, Nicole. Can you believe it? Yeah, that *was* a UFO we saw two nights ago!"

Holding her stomach, Alex rose unsteadily to her feet. "Excuse me, I've got to go to the bathroom."

"Sure," said Robyn. "But hurry back, I've got to put some glitter on your face."

"I'll be right back." Alex shuffled out of Robyn's bedroom and went down the hall. They were on the second floor, and she could hear the doorbell ring downstairs. Robyn's mom answered the door, and tiny voices yelled, "Trick or treat!"

Well, Alex thought, *at least it's still a normal Halloween in Paradise Valley*. She went into the bathroom and shut the door.

When she looked at herself in the mirror, she got a shock. Her face was glowing! That was a common reaction when she was embarrassed, nervous, or losing control of her powers. With all the green makeup, it was hard to tell how much she was glowing, but Alex knew something was wrong. She didn't feel well, and figured that was why she glowed.

What was she going to say to Robyn? She couldn't very well stay in the bathroom all Halloween night. Maybe it would go away quickly, she hoped.

But when she looked again, Alex saw the glow was getting worse! Not only that, but the queasy feeling was spreading to her entire body. She felt light-headed, as if she was about to morph into her liquid state. That wouldn't be so bad, Alex realized. At least then she could escape and get back to Annie—*fast!*

Sure enough, she watched herself in the mirror as she morphed into her full-sized liquid shape. *Okay, now I'll melt into a puddle and get out of here*, she thought, *through a crack in the door or the window.* She could even go down the drain if she wanted to.

But she didn't morph into a puddle. She couldn't do it! Alex was stuck in this in-between shape. She was her normal size, but she was just a quivering, silvery mass on two legs!

CHAPTER 4

A pounding sounded on the bathroom door, and Alex shook like a bowl full of jelly. "Hey," said Robyn, "you've got to listen to the radio. Louis's prank is really taking off!"

"Just a minute!" Alex said. Her voice sounded like a gurgle at the bottom of a well.

"Are you all right?" asked Robyn.

Alex didn't dare answer.

"Okay," said Robyn, "but hurry up. Or we're going to miss all the fun!"

Some fun, Alex thought. She had never been stuck in this condition before, somewhere between human and a puddle of liquid. How long would it last?

35

Alex tried to remain calm. Her only hope was to get home. Her parents were out at a party, and Annie was at the house alone, handing out candy. She was lucky Annie took so much pride in her Halloween duties. Yes, if she could just get home, Annie would know what to do!

But she was on the second floor, and she couldn't flow down the drainpipe. Plus, she was about four blocks away from her house, and the streets were full of trick-or-treaters. How would she get home without being seen?

Luckily, almost everyone out there was in a costume, and it was dark. If anyone saw her, maybe they would think she was just wrapped in aluminum foil.

Alex looked at the bathroom window, knowing that it was her only way out. In her liquid-human shape, she didn't know if she had enough strength to open the window, but she had to try. She put her quivering, jellylike hands around the window jamb and lifted.

The window opened! Whew! It was a good thing that Robyn's family had a newer house. Alex lifted the window all the way, and the cold autumn air flowed around her. When she shivered, her body shook like ripples in a pool of water.

She crawled out the window, hoping there was a tree nearby. Otherwise she would have to jump. *Well, I've got one thing working for me*, she realized. *If I have to jump two stories, at least I won't break any bones.* At the moment, she didn't have any bones!

There was a tree, but it was too far away for her to use. So Alex sat on the windowsill for a moment, looking down at Robyn's side yard. Then she heard voices, as a pack of Halloween ghouls passed by on the sidewalk. Once they were a safe distance, she told herself, "It's now or never."

Alex took a breath of cold air and hurled herself off the windowsill. She landed in a pile of leaves and compressed like a spring, but she shot back up to her regular height. Water, soda, soup, juice, rivers—Alex tried her best to concentrate, but she still couldn't turn into a puddle.

Okay, she was out of Robyn's house and in a dark, eerie suburban world. What would Robyn think when she found her missing? It was too late to leave a note or anything. *Which way should I go?* she wondered. Even though people were in costume, none of them were in a costume like hers. She had to make sure nobody saw her.

Alex had played in these streets ever since she

was a little kid, and she knew all the alleys and the holes in the fences. Her only hope was to sneak around from backyard to backyard, alley to alley.

Again she heard voices out in the street, and quickly hid behind a tree trunk. Panic gripped her churning stomach, but Alex tried to think clearly. There was a row of hedges separating Robyn's backyard from the Mitchells' backyard next door. She remembered a place where she used to squeeze through as a little girl.

Moving through the shadows, Alex crept along the hedge. She found a hole in the bushes where she could sneak through, and she plunged into it. Unfortunately, she wasn't a little girl any-more—she was a big quivering blob—so she got stuck in the thorny branches.

"Ow!" she said in a gurgling voice.

Then a dog began to bark. She didn't remember the Mitchells having a dog! Already halfway through, she had to keep going. Finally, Alex stumbled into the Mitchells' yard just as a bunch of laughing adults stepped out the back door.

"Aahhh!" gasped a woman who was dressed like a princess. "The space alien!"

"Don't vaporize us!" Mr. Mitchell shouted.

"Call the police! Call the army!" another man wailed.

"Yap! Yap!" barked a little cocker spaniel who came charging out.

Alex didn't wait to see what happened next. She smashed through the bushes into the alley, where she hoped she could escape. But there was a pack of kids in gross costumes hanging out, checking their candy. They gaped at her, and a few of them dropped their bags.

"Look at that!" a boy yelled. "Just like on the radio!"

"He'll grab us for weird experiments!" a girl shrieked.

Alex was about to run, but instead *they* all turned and ran, yelling at the top of their lungs. She could hear the voices of the adults in the Mitchells' yard. One of them had a cellular phone and was calling the police. Or maybe it was a radio station.

Whichever it was, Alex knew she was in deep trouble.

As fast as she could, she ran down the alley. Dogs barked at her, and people on the sidewalk were screaming. Alex peered desperately through back fences and clumps of bushes, trying to find a house that looked dark. There had to be some place she could hide. Alex needed a moment to stop and collect her thoughts.

She finally saw a house that looked dark, and it was surrounded by a short brick wall that she could climb over. Alex could hear voices at both ends of the alley, and she knew people were after her. She hated to trespass on someone's property, but she had no choice. If they caught her in this condition, they would never let her go! So Alex grabbed the top of the wall, clambered up, and jumped over.

With a huge splash, she landed in a swimming pool! The cold water chilled her to the bone, except she didn't have any bones. Panting and gasping, Alex paddled to the side of the pool and hauled her dripping, gooey body out.

Then the back porch light came on and the door opened. Alex had no choice—she slid back into the freezing swimming pool. She could only hope that her liquidlike body would blend in with the dark water.

Alex floated silently on top of the water, looking like a weird oil slick. Three men came walking out, one of them with a portable radio which was turned up loud.

"At least ten people have reported seeing the

alien on Birch Street," said an announcer on the radio. "This is no hoax. One of the witnesses was city councilman Arnold Hornsby."

Oh, great! Alex thought.

"I don't see anything out here," said one of the men.

"We've got to catch this creature," another man declared. "It's running around stealing little children!"

"All right, let's form a search party," said the third man. "We'll check every house if we have to. We'll catch that monster."

"Could it be an invasion?" asked the first man.

"Maybe."

"Hey, Joe, you've got to clean your pool. There's something really yucky floating in it."

"Yeah, I know. I'll do it later."

The announcer broke in on the radio: "The chief of police asks that everyone remain calm. Return to your homes, if possible. Do not attempt to apprehend the aliens yourself. Please get off the streets of Paradise Valley and return to your homes."

The three men didn't do as they were told. They went out the back gate, through the fence, and into the alley. Alex was very relieved when she heard the gate clang shut.

By the time she hauled herself out of the freezing swimming pool, she was like a piece of glass. She felt so brittle that she was afraid she would break. Alex huddled in the shadows, trying to get feeling back into her arms and legs.

It didn't help that she could hear a lot of shouting and screaming out in the street. Maybe the police chief had told everyone to remain calm, but they weren't listening.

Panic was in full swing, and Alex Mack was the most panicked one of all.

Annie Mack sat on the living-room couch, reading a chemistry textbook. She wasn't reading it because she had homework—she was reading it for fun. Annie wasn't the type to listen to the radio or watch TV, not when she had a good book to read.

So she had no idea that this wasn't a typical Halloween in Paradise Valley.

The traffic of little ghouls had been fairly heavy early in the evening, but the number had died down in the last half-hour. Annie even felt safe stealing a candy bar out of her bowl.

Annie Mack took her job handing out Halloween candy very seriously. She kept track of how many candy bars she gave away every year, and how many were left; and she adjusted next year's purchases accordingly. She even knew how much candy her parents and Alex stole before Halloween and figured that into her estimate.

If the trick-or-treat traffic didn't pick up, she was going to have lots of candy left over. That bothered Annie. She would have to adjust the figures for next year—or eat the candy herself.

The doorbell rang. *It's about time*, Annie thought. She stood up, grabbed the bowl of candy, and walked to the front door.

When she opened the door, no one yelled, "Trick or treat." The only person there was Robyn, and she looked as if she had been crying. There were streaks in her green makeup, and one of her antennas was bent.

"Annie!" Robyn wailed. "You've got to help me. Alex has been abducted by aliens!"

"What?" asked Annie. "Did you eat too much sugar?"

"No!" Robyn barged into the house. She was wringing her hands, obviously upset. "This is for real, Annie. They're probably looking at her under a microscope right now! Haven't you been listening to the radio or TV?"

"No," Annie answered. "I've been reading and handing out candy."

"Well, turn on the TV!"

"Okay." Annie went to the coffee table and picked up the remote control. "If you're playing a joke on me—"

"It's no joke!" Robyn shrieked. "I mean, it started off as a joke, but it isn't a joke anymore."

Annie tuned the TV to a local channel, and on the screen was an important-looking graphic that read, Special Report!

The announcer came on, looking very grave. "Reports of extraterrestrials landing in Paradise Valley are now confirmed. There have been dozens of sightings all over town, but the most serious sightings have been on Birch Street and the surrounding area."

"That's *our* neighborhood!" Robyn added.

The announcer went on. "UFO sightings were first reported two nights ago, and tonight there were sightings of aliens themselves. They were first reported to a high school radio station in Paradise Valley. Since then, there have been calls to every news outlet in the county.

"The police chief of Paradise Valley has asked for calm. He has requested that all residents return to their homes. Citizens should not—I re-peat, *not*—try to apprehend any suspicious persons themselves. This is a matter for the po-lice and the National Guard."

"National Guard?" Annie looked at Robyn with disbelief. Her mind flashed to the mys-terious Mr. Smith, who lived across the street. He had been very friendly with Alex. But there was something about him that was a little . . . off.

She turned off the TV. "All right, Robyn, why don't you tell me exactly what happened to Alex."

Robyn wrung her hands. "Well, we had just finished calling the radio station to report—"

"Wait a minute—*you* saw the aliens?"

"Well, not exactly. But we didn't know they were real when we reported them."

Annie rubbed her eyes, trying to understand. "Okay, I think we need to start at the begin-ning."

In breathless spurts, Robyn told her about how Louis planned to pull an Orson Welles joke and scare everybody. When Louis's friends called in, none of them knew that there really *were* aliens roaming through town. But afterward, they realized they had all seen the UFO two nights before.

Anyway, it started out as a hoax, but now it was real. Even the TV stations thought so.

"Okay," Annie said calmly, "but when did Alex get abducted by these aliens?"

"I'm coming to that," Robyn said. "She was at my house, and we listened to the show while we were getting dressed. Then we called up Louis and told our stories. Then Nicole called, and Alex went into the bathroom. And I never saw her again!"

Annie breathed a sigh of relief. She didn't say anything, but she knew there could be a logical reason for Alex suddenly disappearing. She could turn liquid and go down the drain, or she could slip out a crack in the window. But why had she left Robyn's house with no explanation?

"Then you didn't actually see any aliens, did you?" she asked.

"No, but lots of other people have seen them," Robyn said.

"There is such a thing as mass hysteria," said Annie. "Throughout history, there have been many recorded incidents of hysteria. If a number of people believe they see something, then more people will believe they've seen it."

"Well, mass hysteria doesn't make people disappear," Robyn pointed out. "And there's something I didn't tell you—the bathroom window was open!"

Annie frowned. In her liquid state, Alex wouldn't need to open a window to leave.

The doorbell rang, and Annie automatically picked up the bowl of candy. "Excuse me, we're still doing the trick-or-treat thing."

But when she opened the door, standing there was Nicole, also wearing green makeup. She was carrying a crude sign that read, Space Visitors, Welcome to Earth!

Nicole spotted Robyn and rushed past Annie to talk to her friend. "Have you seen them?" she asked excitedly. "Are they really here?"

Robyn started crying. "They've got Alex!"

"Oh, that lucky girl," said Nicole. "She's been contacted. The coolest things always happen to her."

"Wait a minute," said Annie. "We don't know if any of this is true. All we know is that Alex was at Robyn's house, and then she left. It doesn't mean she was abducted by aliens."

The front door flew open again, and in rushed George and Barbara Mack. They were dressed like Vikings, with horned helmets, long blond wigs, hairy vests, and big rubber axes.

"What's happening? Is everybody safe?" asked George, pushing a long pigtail off his face.

"Yes, Dad," said Annie. "We're fine."

"No!" Robyn screamed. "The aliens got Alex!"

"They what?" roared George.

Annie rolled her eyes. "Calm down, Dad. Alex is missing, but we don't know—"

"Missing!" Barbara wailed. She rushed for the telephone. "Let's call the police!"

"Hold on, Mom," said Annie. "First of all, this whole alien thing is a hoax."

"No, it's not," Robyn insisted.

Annie glared at her. "I'm telling you, it's a hoax. Robyn, tell them about Louis and his radio show. In fact, tell them *everything*."

In her fractured way, Robyn began the story of Louis and his Orson Welles stunt. Annie couldn't stand to hear it again, so she stepped outside to get some fresh air.

There were still bands of trick-or-treaters on the street. But they weren't going from house to house any longer; they were running in panic. Groups of men carrying baseball bats and crowbars were patrolling the street. Police car sirens were howling in the distance.

Halloween is certainly a mess this year, Annie thought. *All thanks to that idiot, Louis.*

Then she saw something that nearly made her heart stop. Cruising down the street came a huge military vehicle—one of those huge Humvees. Annie was afraid it was the National Guard, until it stopped in front of her and a man poked his head out the window.

It was Vince! That nutcase who used to be head of security at the plant. He had been fired, Annie recalled gleefully. But he still did some freelance work for Danielle Atron, and he was still a nutcase. With his shock of blond hair and cold blue eyes, he was one scary dude.

He leveled her with a steely gaze. "Hey, you're George Mack's kid, aren't you?"

Annie gulped. "Yes."

"Seen any of those aliens running around?"

She shook her head. "No. I think it's a hoax."

"I don't." He took out a metal contraption with a net on the end, and his eyes glittered intensely. "If you see the aliens, I should be informed immediately. We will know how to deal with an alien life-form."

Annie smiled weakly. "Great."

Vince lifted night-vision binoculars to his eyes and stared down the street. "I'd like to get one alive. But if I can't do that—better dead than none at all."

He dropped back into his seat, put the big Humvee into drive, and roared down the street.

"Alex, wherever you are," said Annie, "I hope you're okay. And I hope you stay away from that guy. He's scarier than any alien out there."

CHAPTER 5

Alex sat huddled in the shadows of the strange backyard and tried to warm up. She still heard shouting and sirens. It sounded as if the whole town was going crazy.

She couldn't just sit there and do nothing. Soon the owner of the house would be back. She had to get home and get help from Annie. But she couldn't walk through the streets looking like a big piece of aluminum foil.

Then an idea sparked in her head. What she needed was a costume—a costume that hid all of her body.

Alex stared at the dark house and decided that it looked empty. When the men had left she hadn't heard them lock the door behind them. She hated to break into someone's home, but it wasn't as if she'd never done that before. And this was certainly an emergency if there ever was one.

Usually she could slip into a crack and be gone before anybody noticed her. This time she would have to be more careful, and she would have to be quick. What kind of costume hid everything and was easy to make?

A ghost costume. All she had to do was cut out two holes in a sheet for her eyes, and she could be a ghost. It was risky, but she had to try it. She didn't have much choice.

Screwing up her courage, Alex crept to the back entrance to the house. She pulled the door open and it made a terrible creaking sound. She almost turned back, but she saw something she needed right on the kitchen table—a pair of scissors.

Seeing the scissors spurred her on, and she ducked into the house and grabbed them. She tried to stick the scissors into her pocket, but they slid through her silvery leg and clattered onto the floor. The noise was so loud that it sounded like firecrackers going off!

Nobody came tearing out of the house to grab

her, thankfully. There were still shouts and commotion, but all of that was outside. So she decided to go to the next step and look for a sheet.

She ran down the hall and ducked into the first door that looked like a bedroom. Luckily, it *was* a bedroom. It had a musty smell as if it wasn't used very often, and she figured it was the spare room. There was a big double bed, and she hoped they kept it made.

Alex pulled back the bedspread and breathed a sigh of relief. There was a sheet underneath it! She was beginning to think that her luck had changed for the better when she heard the front door open.

"Come on, guys," said a man's voice. "We'll get something to eat and go back out."

This was no time to be neat. Alex threw off the bedspread, tore the sheet off the mattress, and carried it out of the room. On her way through the kitchen, she scooped the scissors off the floor. Unfortunately, when she rushed out the back door, it creaked loudly again.

"What was that?" the man yelled.

"Somebody's in the house!" another man shouted.

"After them!"

"What if they have phasers?"

Alex didn't wait around to hear more. She went tearing across the backyard, avoiding the pool. She tossed the sheet and scissors over the wall into the alley, then clambered over. As soon as she hit the ground, she heard the door slam open behind her. The men were coming into the yard! It wasn't safe to stay in the alley.

Alex was still near Robyn's house, and she remembered that Robyn's dad had a metal shed in his backyard. He used it to store garbage cans, rakes, and stuff like that. She didn't know if it was locked. It was risky to go back to Robyn's house, but at least she knew her way around there.

She crashed through the bushes into Robyn's backyard. Upstairs, Robyn had left the radio on with the window open, and she could hear Louis's voice:

"Are we having some Halloween, or what?" he asked his listeners. "I want you to know that I, Louis Driscoll, have broken the biggest story ever to hit our fair city. Yes, you heard it here first—that on Halloween night, aliens invaded Paradise Valley."

What a twerp! Alex thought. The next time she saw him, she was going to give him such a zap.

She thought about throwing a stone against

the window to get Robyn's attention. But she didn't want to scare the life out of the poor girl. The way everyone was so panicked and frightened, there was no telling how Robyn would react.

Voices came from the alley, and Alex saw the beam of a flashlight. The men were looking for her!

The voices grew louder as Alex rushed to the metal shed, praying it wasn't locked. As she held her breath, her shimmering hand touched the handle and turned it. The door wasn't locked! As the flashlight beam raked across Robyn's backyard, Alex ducked into the old storage shed.

"Are they in there?" asked a man.

"I don't see them."

With all the junk in the shed, there was barely room for Alex. But she found a place between the garbage can and the lawn mower and sat down. The only light was a faint glow off her face, but she didn't have to do anything too fancy. She found the middle of the sheet and cut two eye holes with the scissors. Her costume was done.

Sheesh, Alex thought, *this is a lot easier than green makeup, hair tint, and rubber ears. Maybe from now on I'll just get an old sheet for Halloween.*

Alex was beginning to feel safe inside the shed, and she wondered if she could just stay hidden there until the effect wore off. Then a police car drove slowly down the alley with its red and blue lights flashing. Luckily, it didn't stop.

No, she couldn't stay behind Robyn's house. It was too close to where everyone had seen the alien. Besides, she didn't know if the effect would ever wear off. She had to get home!

Also, listening to Louis on the radio was driving her crazy.

Screwing up her courage again, Alex slipped out of the shed. She threw the sheet over her head and felt a little safer. *Okay, now I don't look that much different from other kids out on Halloween.*

It seemed like a very long night, but it had probably only been thirty or forty minutes since her problems first started. She heard voices in the Mitchells' yard next door, and it sounded as if they were talking to the police. Alex knew she had to get away from Birch Street.

Taking a deep breath, she plowed through the bushes back into the alley. With a jolt, she realized that her costume wasn't really complete because she didn't have a bag for trick-or-treating. Then Alex remembered that she had frightened a bunch of kids in the alley. Some of them had dropped their bags when they ran. She hurried to the end of the alley and looked around.

To her relief, she found an old pillowcase and some squashed candy on the ground. It was enough for her disguise. Alex quickly scooped the candy into the pillowcase and walked into the street. She was careful to keep her hands covered by the sheet.

Reaching the sidewalk was really scary, because there were police cars and frightened people everywhere. Nobody was going to stay home on a night when Paradise Valley was being invaded by aliens. There was comfort in numbers, and people stood around in small groups. Some of them were talking, but most of them were looking suspiciously at each other.

Who was a human, and who was an alien?

Fortunately, a lot of people were still in costume, and Alex tried to blend in. She wanted to be just another ghost with a bag of Halloween candy. Carefully, she avoided the bright lights of the streetlamps.

It would look suspicious if she ran, so Alex walked very slowly. Besides, she couldn't see all that well through the small holes she had cut in the sheet.

"I say we go house to house!" one man was telling a woman police officer. "We've got to find these aliens!"

"I know," said the officer. "But we have laws against dragging people out of their houses." She turned to the gathered crowd. "How many of you actually saw the aliens? Raise your hands."

Alex stopped to see the response. Only a few hands went up.

"And what exactly were they doing?" the policewoman inquired. "And don't tell me anything you didn't actually see."

One of the teenagers frowned in thought. "Um, this alien was—it was just standing there."

"Did it actually attack anyone?"

"No, it ran away."

The police officer nodded. "That doesn't sound very threatening, does it? Are you sure it wasn't just somebody in a Halloween costume?"

The teenager laughed nervously. "If that was a costume, I'd like to have one!"

No you wouldn't, Alex thought. She turned around and promptly ran into the chest of a large man.

"Excuse me," he said. "Are you all right?"

Alex gave him a big nod, because she couldn't

talk. Her voice would gurgle as if she were standing at the bottom of a well.

"You might as well get home," said the man. "Halloween is over for tonight."

She nodded again and hurried away from the man. With police cars and crowds gathered on the street, no one was paying much attention to her. Alex hoped it would stay that way.

But some *thing* was following her. And it wasn't human. She only got a glimpse of it out of the corner of her eye, but it followed her all the way down the block.

As Alex rounded the corner, she breathed a huge sigh of relief and leaned against a tree. Just getting away from Robyn's street, where the alien had been spotted, was a big step. In her ghost costume, she felt confident that she could make it home without anyone stopping her.

That was when the *thing* moved in.

"Yap! Yap! Yap!" barked the little dog, nipping at her heels.

At first she didn't recognize the dog. Then she realized it was the Mitchells' cocker spaniel. In all the commotion, it must have gotten loose from their backyard.

"Go away!" she whispered, walking at a fast pace. "Get out of here!"

But the little dog knew who the alien was. It followed her down the sidewalk. "Yap! Yap! Grrrr! Grrrr!"

Nervously, Alex looked around. There were people sitting on their front porches and looking out their windows. She couldn't tell if they had noticed her yet, but they were going to, if the stupid dog didn't stop.

Worse yet, a big military vehicle—a Humvee—rounded the corner and stopped in front of her. It looked like Vince's car.

Suddenly, the dog grabbed the sheet between its teeth and yanked it off her head! With its tail wagging proudly, the dog ran down the street with her costume.

And standing in the middle of the sidewalk— in all its shimmering glory—was the alien of Paradise Valley!

"Bingo!" Vince yelled. With his tires squealing, he floored the gas pedal of his Humvee and sped toward her!

CHAPTER 6

In the living room of the Mack house, George Mack listened to Robyn's cockeyed story. Annie had never seen her father look quite so angry. He banged his rubber ax on the floor and tossed his blond Viking braids.

"That's a very irresponsible trick to pull on this town," George said crossly. "It seems clear to me that Annie is right—this whole thing is a hoax. Don't you know that people get panicked easily, especially after all those movies about spacemen invading earth?"

Nicole frowned, looking hurt. "How come nobody told *me* about Louis's plan?"

"It's a typical case of mass hysteria," said

Annie. "Look at Robyn—even the people who *started* the hoax now believe it! I'm going to write a paper about this for my psychology class."

"There are mobs roaming the streets and police cars tearing around," said George. "Everyone is scared out of his wits. Someone could get hurt. You kids have ruined Halloween for everybody!"

Robyn bowed her head and looked miserable. "I'm sorry, Mr. Mack. We shouldn't have done it."

"You're darn right," said George, "and now we're going to correct the problem. Annie, turn on the radio and tune it to the high school station."

"Good idea." She rushed to the stereo and tuned in Louis's broadcast. His conceited voice filled the airwaves.

"Don't worry, folks," said Louis, "as long as I'm around, you have nothing to worry about. If you don't get abducted by aliens tonight, you have *me* to thank for it. I was the one who warned the whole town about the alien invasion. If any of the TV stations or newspapers would like to interview me, my name is Louis Driscoll. You can call me here at the station, 555-4388."

"We'll call him all right," said George. He picked up the telephone and dialed.

"Here's another phone call now," Louis said smugly. "Hello, caller, how many aliens have you seen tonight?"

"None," George answered, "because there aren't any aliens."

Louis chuckled. "I don't know how you can say that. Haven't you been listening to my show?"

"No, but I have been talking to your friends, like Robyn. And I know that you put them up to calling in and reporting fake aliens and fake UFOs."

"Heh-heh." Louis's nervous laugh beamed all over Paradise Valley. "Sorry, caller, I've got to move on to some other callers now—"

"You'd better not, Louis. This is George Mack, Alex's father, and I know my daughter was in on this stupid prank. I'll deal with her later. Does the name 'Orson Welles' mean anything to you?"

"Uh, um . . . I think we need to play a little music—"

"No, you don't. You need to tell people the *truth*. And I want you to call up the other TV and radio stations and tell them the truth, too."

"Okay, Mr. Mack," Louis said glumly. "But

not everybody calling in was my friend. How do you explain all those other people who think they saw aliens?''

"I don't know, and I don't care. The point is, we've got to correct the damage you've done. I didn't think it was possible to ruin Halloween, but you did it!''

"I'm sorry," Louis said over the air. "I thought we might fool a few people for ten minutes. I promise, I'll keep broadcasting that it's a hoax. Just like Orson Welles did in 1938.''

"Keep it simple, Louis. Good-bye." George turned off the radio.

Barbara Mack smiled proudly at her husband and tugged at one of his long braids. "That was very good, George.''

"Thank you." He straightened his Viking helmet.

"But we still don't know where Alex is," Mrs. Mack said, her brow creasing.

"Yeah." He frowned. "Robyn, is there anything you forgot to tell us?''

"Well," Robyn said, "Alex didn't really think this prank was a good idea. She wanted to back out of it.''

"Oh," said George, "Alex has some sense after

all. So maybe she sneaked out to tell people it wasn't real. Maybe she felt guilty."

"That's probably it," Annie said quickly. "Listen, Dad, why don't you, Mom, Robyn, and Nicole go out and look for Alex. I bet she's somewhere in the neighborhood. While you're out there, you can tell people the story is a fake."

"Okay," Mr. Mack said, and began ushering everybody toward the door. "What are you going to do?"

Annie shrugged. "Somebody should stay here, in case Alex shows up."

"Good idea," he said. "You tell her to stay home. She's grounded!"

Looking like a very strange band, two green space aliens and two blond Vikings filed out the door together.

Annie shut the door behind them and breathed a sigh of relief. Maybe they didn't think that Alex was in real trouble, but Annie wasn't so sure. She had a new theory about what had happened to her little sister.

If Alex had put on all that green makeup, hair tint, and glitter, she might have altered her body chemistry. Maybe she had started glowing, or even worse. That would give her good reason to leave Robyn's house with no explanation.

Annie didn't even want to think about it, but she feared that Alex was the "alien" that so many people had seen. That made it even more dangerous that Vince was out there in the streets, looking for the space beings.

Plus, there was Mr. Smith across the street. How did he figure in all this?

The doorbell rang again, and Annie picked up the bowl of candy and went to the door. If these were trick-or-treaters, tonight was their lucky night. There were still lots of candy bars to give away.

She opened the door and Ray was standing there, dressed in his regular clothes. He looked down at the bowl and grabbed a candy bar. "Thank you, don't mind if I do."

Annie grabbed his arm and hauled him inside. "Have you seen Alex?" she demanded.

"No, I've been looking all over for her, but it's a little crazy out there. I even went home and changed."

She glared at him. "Your friend Louis has caused a lot of trouble tonight."

"Oh," said Ray, looking guilty. "You know about that, huh? I guess we did scare a few people. I didn't know I was such a good actor."

Annie scowled. "You're not. I have everything

figured out, except where Alex is. Listen, you stay here in case she comes home. Check the garage—she would go there."

"Where are you going?"

"I'm not sure." She grabbed her jacket and rushed for the door. "And don't eat all the candy!"

Ray jerked his hand out of the bowl and said, "Okay."

Panting for breath, Alex dashed down another alley. People were shouting and a mob was chasing her. But she was more worried about the headlights from Vince's Humvee and the police cars circling the neighborhood.

She heard the screech of tires and saw red and blue lights flashing at the end of the alley. It was a police car! Vince was roaring toward her from the other end, and a frightened mob of people were charging through backyards, yelling at each other.

Alex stopped for a moment and tried to figure out where she was. She was one block closer to home than she had been, but she was still three long blocks away. Desperately she looked around to see if she recognized anything.

She was near the Johnsons' backyard—she recognized it from the old tree house. There was a tall chain-link fence that would take forever to climb over. But if they hadn't fixed it, there was a hole in the bottom of the fence. As kids, they had often crawled through the hole on their way to the tree house.

Vince squealed to a stop about twenty feet away from her. "I've got you now!" he shouted. "You space monster!"

As he leveled his weapon at her, Alex dropped to her hands and knees and scurried for the fence. The hole was still there! She squeezed through just as a blast from his high-tech toy chewed up a mound of dirt.

"Hold it right there!" the police shouted from the other end of the alley.

"Darn it!" Vince growled. He threw the Humvee into reverse and peeled down the alley, away from the cops.

Alex had ditched him for the moment, but there were still twenty other people chasing her. She ran through the Johnsons' backyard, trying to think of all the places she had played as a kid.

Drainage pipes! Every time it rained, the Johnsons had trouble with flooding in their backyard. So they put in some drainage pipes that channeled the water down into the storm drains.

When she was a kid, the pipes had been just big enough to crawl through. She only hoped she could still get into them.

"The monster went this way!" someone yelled.

As the shouts got louder, she saw a group of people come running around the side of the Johnsons' house. There was no time to think! Alex dove to her stomach and inched her way through the bushes like a silver caterpillar.

She reached the drainage pipe just as a mob of people filled up the Johnsons' backyard. Alex squirmed into the nearest pipe, hoping she wouldn't get stuck. The stench was pretty bad inside. She tried to hold her nose, but her face was like jelly.

"The alien was just here!" someone shouted. "I think I saw it go in those bushes!"

"What did it look like?" a curious voice asked.

"I don't know—sort of shiny. I think it was wearing a space suit."

"Yeah, that's it!" someone else shouted. "The alien is wearing a space suit. It can't breathe in our atmosphere!"

Alex stifled a cough. She was having a hard time breathing in the atmosphere of the old drainage pipe. But she didn't dare move, sneeze, or cough.

"What's going on here?" a voice demanded. Alex recognized it as the voice of the woman police officer.

"We're chasing the alien!" a man cried. "It came right through here."

"Listen," said the policewoman, "we just got a report that this whole thing is a hoax. It was all cooked up by that deejay on the high school radio station."

"What?" someone protested. "You can't be serious. We *saw* it!"

"I don't know what you saw, but if you turn on the radio station, you'll hear the deejay talking about it. He's apologizing for the trouble he's caused."

"It's a cover-up!" someone shouted.

"Yeah, it's a cover-up!" several voices agreed.

"The FBI doesn't want us to know the truth!"

"The president is an alien!"

"Okay," said the cop angrily, "that's it! Do any of you actually *live* in this house?"

For the first time, the mob was silent.

"I didn't think so," the officer said. "I could arrest all of you for trespassing, destroying property, and making a public nuisance. You people are more of a danger than a hundred aliens!"

Alex sighed. What luck! The cops were coming to her rescue, although they didn't know it.

"If you don't disperse right now, I'm going to run you all in," the officer continued.

Grumbling among themselves, the crowd of people wandered off. But Alex was sure that they wouldn't wander too far, because they were still convinced the alien invasion was real.

She saw the beam of a flashlight cutting through the bushes and realized the cops had started looking for her. Alex held her breath to make herself smaller and crawled deeper into the yucky drainpipe. The flashlight beam shined into the opening of the pipe, and Alex scurried faster.

"Who's in there?" a cop demanded.

Alex didn't dare answer—she just kept crawling into the drain, hoping the cops were too large too follow. It was sure a lot easier to go through a drain in liquid form than her slimy in-between state.

Because her face was still glowing, she had a faint light to guide her. As she burrowed deeper, Alex could see only a few inches ahead of her and she had no idea where she was going. Even as a kid, she had never crawled so far into these old pipes.

It was too narrow to turn back—she had to keep going straight ahead. What if there were snakes, rats, racoons, or other weird animals in the pipe? *Well, if they see me like this, they'll probably be scared stiff,* she told herself.

Suddenly the pipe sloped downward and she started to slide forward on the old leaves and mud. Alex tried to stop her descent, but she was soon flying through the pipe as if she were on a water slide.

"Help!" Alex warbled, going faster and faster.

Without warning, the pipe disappeared beneath her and she plunged into the darkness!

CHAPTER 7

Annie Mack was desperate. She didn't know where to turn. What she was about to do was a long shot, but she didn't know what else to do. So she lifted her fist and knocked on the front door of the house.

A small figure peeked through the blinds of the living-room window. "Go away! There's no more candy!"

"Sorry to bother you, Mrs. Brownstein, but it's me, Annie Mack. I live across the street."

"How do I know it's really *you?*" the old woman asked. "Those space people can look like anybody they want!"

Annie took a deep breath and tried to sound

calm. "Please believe me. It's really me. Remember how I used to sell you Girl Scout cookies? Your favorite kind are Thin Mints."

"Okay, you know that much," said Mrs. Brownstein. "But what if the aliens have taken over your body? What if you're one of those *pod people?* What if you have one of those pods with you, and you're going to put it under my bed?"

Annie rubbed her eyes. She didn't need this. Raising her hands palms up in front of her, she said, "Mrs. Brownstein, I don't have anything in my hands. I'm not going to leave anything under your bed. In fact, the whole alien invasion is a hoax. It's something the deejay on the high school radio station made up."

Finally Annie heard a bunch of bolts and locks turning, and the door creaked open. With a kindly smile, Mrs. Brownstein ushered her into the house. The furnishings were old and dusty, and the house hadn't changed much since Annie was a little girl.

"I never believed that nonsense, anyway," said the small white-haired woman. "Why would space people want to look like *us?*"

"That's a good question," Annie answered. "Have you seen my sister, Alex?"

Mrs. Brownstein looked thoughtful. "Well,

there were many children here earlier this evening before the scare. How was she dressed?"

"You probably haven't seen her," said Annie. "Is your boarder, Mr. Smith, here?"

"Such a nice man. So polite and quiet." The woman gasped. "You don't think *he* could be an alien, do you?"

"No," Annie lied. "Believe me, there aren't any aliens at all. You should turn on the high school radio station and listen for yourself."

Mrs. Brownstein smiled sweetly. "I will, dearie. If you want to see Mr. Smith, his room is at the top of the stairs. He hasn't been out all night."

Smart man, Annie thought. "Thank you."

Slowly, Annie climbed the stairs. She almost felt like running in the opposite direction. How silly was it to think that a nice, polite stranger like Mr. Smith was a man from outer space? She was no better than those crazed people running around on the streets.

At the top of the stairs she stopped. This was ridiculous—she wasn't going to bother him. Annie turned to go back down the stairs when a door opened behind her.

"Miss Mack?" asked a cultured voice.

Annie whirled around to see Mr. Jonathan

Smith standing in the doorway of his room. As usual, he was dressed in a dark suit and tie, and his gray hair was neatly combed. Annie got a slight chill down her spine.

"You wanted to see me?" he asked.

Annie nodded. "If I'm not intruding."

"Not at all," said Mr. Smith. "Please come in."

He stepped back from the door and allowed her to enter. It was a simple room with a chest of drawers, a desk, a bed, and not much else. On the bed was a suitcase that was half packed.

"Are you leaving?" she asked.

"I'm afraid so. I can't say that the chemical plant was very cooperative. I was going to leave this morning, but Alex suggested that I stay and watch Halloween." He glanced out his bedroom window. "In Paradise Valley, Halloween is a very exciting holiday."

"Yeah," said Annie, "this year it was exciting, all right. Mr. Smith, it was Alex that I wanted to talk about. Have you seen her tonight?"

"No." Smith looked concerned. "She hasn't run into trouble, has she?"

Annie shrugged. "Probably not. It's just that she's missing, and there's been so much craziness tonight. Some kids started a rumor that we

had been invaded by people from outer space."
She laughed nervously.

"I see," Mr. Smith answered. "I wouldn't
worry about Alex too much. She's a very special girl."

"That's what I think, too." Annie held out her
hand. "It's been a pleasure to meet you, Mr.
Smith. If you ever come back—"

"That's not likely. But if I see Alex, I'll send
her home." He shook her hand, and his grip felt
cool and dry.

"Thank you." Annie stepped out into the hall-
way, and he shut the door behind her.

Well, that was certainly a waste of time, Annie
thought, frustrated. No closer to finding out
what had happened to Alex, she decided to go
home and wait for her sister's return.

After sliding down the drainpipe, Alex went
spinning through the darkness, only to land in
an underground pool of freezing water. She shot
to the surface, gasping for breath. Dirty, brackish
water swirled all around her and she clawed at
the walls to get out.

Stay calm, she ordered herself. The water
wasn't over her head, and she found that she
could stand up. As badly as she wanted to get

out of there, it wouldn't do any good to panic. At least she was safe from Vince, the crowds, and the police—for the moment.

Working from one end of the pool to the other, Alex felt along the wall, looking for something to grab. Finally she found the rungs of a ladder, and she dragged herself out of the water like a seal lumbering its way onto land.

When Alex staggered to the level above her, she bumped her head on a low concrete ceiling. "Ow!" she gurgled. She looked around, using the faint glow from her face as light. Alex found herself surrounded by pipes, all emptying into the reservoir. These pipes came from the street and were larger than the one she had been in— about four feet wide.

Alex found that she could stand in these drainage pipes if she hunched over like a crab. But at least it was dry and fairly warm in this part of the underground maze.

Hmmm, Alex thought, *maybe falling down here was a lucky break in disguise*. The storm drains had openings near roads and washes all over the neighborhood. If she knew where the drains went, she could use them to get home, or close to home.

Unfortunately, she didn't know which way

the drains went. And she had a lousy sense of direction.

Wait a minute, Alex thought. She had a lousy sense of direction when she was a regular human; when she was a liquid blob, she had a great sense of direction. She knew instinctively which way to go when surging through a dark bathroom drain.

At the moment, she was midway between two shapes—neither blob nor human—so she figured she had an okay sense of direction. Alex thought about where the Johnsons' house was in relation to her own. Maybe one of these pipes let out in that big ditch at the end of her street.

With a sigh, she picked a direction and hoped for the best. The pipe had to come out somewhere on the surface. Slowly, scrunched over, Alex did a crab walk down the long, dark passageway.

If I could only get through this, Alex thought, *I'd never go out on Halloween again. I'll stay home and hand out candy, just like Annie. There's no place like home for Halloween! There's no place like home for Halloween!*

After five minutes of trying to walk, she was exhausted. She got down on her hands and knees and crawled for a while. The rumble of cars passing overhead told her she was under a street.

Suddenly she heard voices, and she almost ran in terror. But the voices were faint, and she realized they were far overhead. She was probably crawling under a sidewalk. Even though nobody could see her moving underground, Alex scurried away from the voices. Ahead of her, the drainpipe took a sudden curve to the right.

After rounding the curve, Alex could see a faint glow of light ahead of her. Thinking she was close to getting out, she plunged toward the golden glow.

After a few more feet, she was surprised to learn that the light didn't come from the street. It came from a small flashlight lying in the tunnel next to a pile of blankets. *That's odd*, Alex thought. *Why would anybody leave a flashlight on down here?*

She felt like turning back, but there was nothing behind her but that dank pool of water. If nobody else wanted the flashlight, she figured she could use it. Slowly, Alex crept toward the objects that had been left inside the pipe.

The flashlight glimmered weakly, and she reached to pick it up. Suddenly the pile of blankets shifted and a grizzled face peered out at her.

Alex tried to scream, but it came out like a strangled groan. The man in the blankets had no such trouble—he screamed loudly.

"Help! Help!" He scurried away from her. "Don't eat me!"

"Stop!" she said clearly enough.

The man stopped and stared at her. He had to be a homeless man who had been forced to sleep in the drainage pipe. She felt sorry for him, but she couldn't turn back—she had to get past him.

He blinked at her in amazement. "What *are* you?"

"I'm . . . I'm the Guardian of the Sewers!" she announced in a gurgle.

His eyes widened, and he looked impressed. "I didn't know sewers had guardian spirits."

"Well, now you know. Tell me, where does this pipe open up?"

"You're the Guardian of the Sewers, and you don't know where they go?" He stared at her suspiciously.

"There are so many," Alex answered, "I sometimes forget." At least this fellow hadn't heard about the alien invasion. She guessed that news didn't get down to the sewers very fast.

Grabbing his blankets, he crawled toward her.

"This tube comes out on Redstone Road, under the overpass."

"Good," Alex said. "I mean, thank you. I'm going to leave you here, and I don't want you to tell anyone about me."

"Who would I tell?" he asked.

"No one!" she warned him with her strange voice. She quickly shuffled past him.

"Is it . . . is it all right if I sleep here?" he asked.

"You'll get sick if you try to stay all winter down here. You know, there are people who could find you food and shelter. You really should ask for their help."

"I will!" he answered, nodding. "What are you? Like, a being of pure energy? An elemental spirit?"

"I'm your worst nightmare."

"No, you're not *my* worst nightmare. I think you're sort of cool." He pointed down the long, dark pipe. "Keep going, you'll get out."

She scuttled away from the homeless man. As she moved along the pipe, it began to slope upward—that was an encouraging sign. Behind her, she could hear the man talking, although he had to be talking to himself. Who else?

The going was slow, scuttling through the

pipe, but Alex could tell she was headed upward. The rumble of cars overhead told she was under a street, probably Redstone Road. The eerie groaning of the asphalt was even louder than before. She had to be getting closer to the surface. If her calculations were correct, she would emerge about two blocks from her house. Despite the dangers above her, Alex wanted to be out in the fresh air again. More than anything, she just wanted to be home, cuddled up in her bed.

She plunged on, ever upward, and finally saw a sliver of blue light ahead of her. It was no more than moonlight, but it looked great to Alex. She surged forward, trying to ignore the aches and the weariness.

The sound of vehicle tires churning overhead was just a few feet away. She could see moonlight in the ditch ahead of her, and knew she would be coming out on the far side of the wash. She would have to find a way to cross the road without being seen to get back home.

Alex clawed her way out of the drainage pipe, anxious for freedom. As soon as she staggered into the fresh air, she heard a pop and whirled around just as a thick net of rope and metal slammed into her. It wrapped around her like an octopus!

Under the weight of the net, Alex dropped to the concrete, struggling to get out. She kept thrashing around on the sidewalk. No matter what she did, there was no escape.

Through her panic Alex heard a triumphant voice say, "Hold it right there, spaceman. You're under arrest for invading our planet!"

Vince! Alex twisted around and saw him hop down from the top of the drainage pipe. He was holding a radio and grinning from ear to ear.

He spoke into the device, "Home Plate to Jackson—you did a great job. We got our alien! All my operatives can come in from their posts. I repeat, all operatives come in. Good thing I called you boys—I needed the extra manpower. This is Home Plate, out."

Vince crossed his arms and smiled down at Alex. "Hey, alien, you know how you people like studying humans? Well, we're gonna see how *you* like being a science experiment. We're gonna find out everything about you."

Alex twisted and turned. She tried to scream, but the sound came out as a helpless gurgle.

CHAPTER 8

At the Mack house, Annie paced a path on the living room carpet. Ray sat on the couch, looking first at his watch, then at the bowl of candy.

"Are you going to do anything?" Annie asked.

"Well," said Ray, "I'd eat a candy bar if you'd let me."

"Go ahead and eat them all! What about Alex? What about the panic out there?"

Ray quickly opened a candy bar. "Annie, you know it's all a joke. So what are you worried about?"

"Those people didn't take it as a joke, and lots of them are convinced they actually *saw* something. Plus, Vince is out there looking for spacemen. And where *is* Alex? Four people are searching, and they haven't been able to find her."

"Okay, okay." Ray rose to his full lanky height. "I'll go look. But I don't think you should worry so much. Alex is pretty good at staying hidden, if she wants to. She's probably found a safe hideout."

"I know. Good luck."

A loud knock sounded on the door, and Annie rushed in that direction, saying, "Maybe this will be good news."

She opened the door, and three tough-looking men muscled their way past her and into the house. They started looking around, behind curtains and in closets.

"Hey, have you seen any aliens from outer space?" the leader asked. "They're silvery, mushy kind of critters."

"How dare you barge in here!" Annie protested. "Get out at once."

One of them looked suspiciously at Ray. "We're only trying to protect you."

"Who are you guys?" Ray asked. "If you're police, show your badges."

"We're concerned citizens, that's all," said the leader. He glanced around and didn't see anything unusual. Then he thrust a business card into Annie's hand. "If you see anything, call this number. I'm not kidding—these creatures are real! And they're not even close to being human."

"Yeah, we captured one of 'em!" said the youngest one.

The other two men glared at him, and the young thug gulped.

"That's not common knowledge," said the leader. "I'd appreciate it if you would forget you heard that."

Annie charged to the phone and picked up the receiver. "I'm going to call the police."

"No need, we're going." The leader shoved the other two out the door. "Remember what I told you—they're real." He stepped outside and slammed the door.

"I can't get through," Annie said after dialing. "The police line is busy. All the calls must have crashed the system."

"All right," Ray said, looking worried. "Now I think we *do* have to look for her. Where do we start?"

"Let's check the radio station first," said Annie. "It's a long shot, but maybe she went to school to see Louis."

She turned up the stereo, and Louis's voice came over the air sounding hoarse and tired. "Listen, everybody, you can relax," he said. "It's all over. We got caught—I confess to what I did. The whole alien story is a hoax. Why won't anybody listen to me?"

The phone rang in the studio, and he answered it. "Hello? Do you have something to say?"

"I sure do," said an angry male voice. "We won't listen to you because you're an idiot. Half the town has seen the space invaders, but you don't believe it. Get with the program!"

"I don't *have* to believe it," Louis said wearily. "I started the story in the first place. I *am* the program!"

"Oh, now you're trying to take credit for something someone else did," the caller scoffed. "You're probably part of the cover-up."

"There's no cover-up!" Louis insisted. "I'm telling you the truth. Nobody needs to do a cover-up, because the story was fake to begin with."

"Kids nowadays never believe their elders," the man grumbled. "When the aliens grab you and put you in a space zoo—don't come crying to me!" Loudly, he hung up.

Instantly the phone rang again, and groaning, Louis answered it. "Hello, this is Paradise High School. Caller, I hope *you* believe this was all a hoax."

"Oh, I believe it all right," said a stern voice. "Louis, this is your principal speaking."

Louis's moan echoed all over town, and Annie turned off the stereo. "It doesn't sound as if Alex is there."

"Yes, he's definitely alone," said Ray. "I think Louis's days as a deejay are over."

"We can't just sit here." Annie grabbed her jacket and her purse and headed for the door.

Ray rushed after her. "Where are we going?"

"I don't know yet."

Annie and Ray strolled along the sidewalk, trying to look as if they were hanging out, like so many other people. With the rumored alien invasion, nobody seemed to want to go home and be alone. They wanted to be out in the streets, among others of their kind.

A lot of people were still dressed in Halloween costumes, which gave the gathering a festive air. Some folks were laughing about the invasion, and others stared at the gathering people as if they didn't think they were really human. The invasion might have been phony, but the fright was real. People didn't know whom to trust.

When a police car came streaking through with its sirens blaring, Annie got the shivers. In all the insanity, how did she expect to find Alex? She didn't even know where to look for her sister.

She was about to tell Ray that they might as well go home, when she spotted something. It was the three men who had barged into her home! They were making their way slowly down the street, stopping often to talk to people. She grabbed Ray's arm, turned him around, and walked away from the men.

"What is it?" he whispered.

"Those three thugs who crashed our house—they're just ahead of us. See them talking to the people on the front porch of that house?"

Ray's jaw tightened. "You know, I'd like to tell them a thing or two. Excuse me."

"No, wait," she said, pulling him back. "If we follow them, they might lead us to Alex."

"Do you really think they caught her?" Ray asked.

Annie shrugged. "All I know is that they caught *something*, and Alex is missing."

"But they're moving so slowly," said Ray. "Won't they spot us?"

"That's a problem," Annie agreed, looking around. "What we need are Halloween costumes."

Ray blinked at her in amazement. "I just took my costume off. Besides, I thought *you* never wore a Halloween costume."

"Tonight I'll make an exception," said Annie. "We have to follow those men and see where they go."

She looked up and down the street until she spotted two small boys sitting on the curb, sorting their candy. Their parents were probably looking frantically for them, but they were as happy as ducks in a pond. On the ground beside them were two discarded plastic masks.

"Keep an eye on the men," Annie told Ray. "I'll be right back."

As Annie walked toward the boys, she opened her purse and checked the money in her wallet. She had a bunch of one-dollar bills, which she hoped would be enough.

"Hi, guys," she said in a friendly fashion. "You did very well. That's a lot of candy."

The boys looked suspiciously at her. "And you can't have any of it," warned one of them.

She frowned. "It's too bad that trick-or-treating had to end so early tonight."

"Yeah," agreed the smallest boy. "It's all the fault of those stupid aliens. Why did they have to come on Halloween? Why not Valentine's Day?"

"Or my birthday," said the other one.

Annie glanced over her shoulder and saw Ray waving to her. She had to get to the point.

"You probably won't need those masks anymore tonight," she told the boys. "So listen. My friend and I have got to go to a costume party, and we don't have any costumes. Would you like to sell me your masks? I'll give you three dollars apiece."

The boys stared at one another. "Three dollars!" they shrieked in unison. "Okay!"

Annie paid the boys and grabbed her masks, without taking a close look at them. She rushed back to Ray, who was edging down the sidewalk.

"The men started moving faster," he said. "They're going around that corner."

"I see them." As they chased after the thugs, Annie checked her two masks. "Oh, no."

"What is it?"

She held up the goofy masks. "Do you want to be Ren or Stimpy?"

Looking like a ball of aluminum foil wrapped in rubber bands, Alex sat in the cargo bed of Vince's Humvee. She struggled against the heavy net, but it was no use. Unless she could morph into a liquid, she wasn't going to get out of the worst mess she'd ever been in in her entire life.

Jackson, the man she had met in the drainage pipe, sat in the passenger seat beside Vince. He kept glancing back at Alex, giving her disgusted looks, as if he'd never seen anything so horrible. *What a scuzzball he is, pretending to be a homeless person. Vince and his buddies don't fight fair*, she thought angrily.

Alex wondered where they were going, although she knew it couldn't be the chemical plant. Vince couldn't get in there since Danielle Atron had fired him.

"It talks, you know," Jackson told Vince. "Not very well, but it told me it was the Guardian of the Sewers!"

Vince let loose a raspy laugh. "Maybe that's what we'll call the best-selling book I'm gonna write about it: *The Guardian of the Sewers*." Then he frowned. "Wait a minute, what if the aliens have a whole underground hive built in the sewer system? What if that space creature *is* the Guardian of the Sewers!"

Vince wheezed in horror and pounded on Jackson's arm. "What if it's after the GC-161 kid? Did you think of that!"

Alex groaned, and it came out a gurgle. She had been captured by the one person to whom she couldn't possibly tell the truth. This was a big day for Vince, the biggest day in his life—and the absolute worst day in hers. He had finally caught the GC-161 kid, but he didn't know it!

If she hadn't been so scared, she would have laughed about it.

Jackson looked at Alex with a pained expression. "That's a weird one, all right. For this cargo, you could get some serious money."

Vince seemed to be thinking the same thing. "Yeah, I don't know why I should take it to Ms. Atron. She fired me, so why do I owe her any loyalty? Maybe I should just sell it to the highest bidder. Lots of governments would pay plenty for a genuine extraterrestrial."

"Not only that," said Jackson, "but crazy billionaires, rock musicians, all kinds of people would want it. And after we sell a real one of these, we could probably sell a dozen fake ones. You're sitting on a gold mine, Vince."

The vehicle thudded over a pothole, causing Alex to bounce painfully in the cargo bed. If she didn't do something fast, she would be on her way to a laboratory to be sliced and diced. Or she'd wind up floating in a big bottle full of smelly chemicals, like aliens in the movies. *Nicole was right*, Alex thought. *Aliens should be treated with much more kindness and respect.*

Alex knew she couldn't liquefy herself all the way. She had been trying to morph every few minutes, and it didn't work. But she had other talents. Until being captured, she had been afraid to try her other powers, such as zapping and telekinesis. Maybe some of them worked—but in strange ways, like her morphing ability. There was no way to find out unless she tried, and Alex was getting desperate.

She worked a silver finger between the ropes of the net and pointed at Vince's dashboard. With all her will, Alex began to concentrate. If she could make his gas gauge look empty, he'd be forced to pull over and stop.

Much to her complete surprise, a lightning bolt shot from her finger and, like a photon torpedo, exploded the dashboard! The steering wheel broke off in Vince's hands and smoke poured into his face. The Humvee swerved back and forth, totally out of control.

"Look out!" Jackson screamed in horror. "The monster has laser beams!"

Vince kept turning the steering wheel, even though it wasn't attached to anything. "We're gonna crash!" he yelled.

He hit the brakes, the tires squealed, and the car lurched into a spin. Both men screamed and Alex gurgled as the Humvee hurtled off the road into a ditch.

CHAPTER 9

Omigosh, I have a super zap! Alex thought. This was her last thought before the Humvee spun off the road. As they plunged into the ditch, Alex bounced around in the back like a rubber ball. Finally the vehicle pitched over, and she was tossed against the roll bars. "Ooomph!" she groaned.

With its wheels spinning, the vehicle came to a stop. It was lying on its side in a ditch beside a lonely country road.

Vince and Jackson hung in their seat belts, dazed and moaning. They didn't look badly hurt. Alex rolled over and felt dirt clods under her body. The sides and back of the Humvee were wide open. She could just crawl out the window and escape, if only she wasn't trapped in the stupid net!

Vince moaned, and Alex knew that he would be back to his usual cheery self in a few seconds. Despite the danger of her super zap, she had no choice but to use it again. She had to get out of the net!

Alex spread her fingers and unleashed an explosion of sparks that lit up the vehicle like a comet. The net melted and sizzled away, and so did much of the car. Vince and Jackson were suddenly wide awake! They started screaming and trying to crawl over each other to get out the side door.

Alex crawled out the back window. She tried to stand up and fell down twice. It felt as if all her muscles and nerves were shot. One thing was sure—she couldn't use her super zap for anything but dire emergencies. *Though I wouldn't mind giving Louis a super zap if I ever get out of this mess,* she thought wryly.

Shuffling like a blob on two feet, Alex managed to stagger away from the wrecked car. Beside her, part of the ditch blew up, and she dove to the ground. She looked back to see Vince with one of his high-tech weapons.

"Hey, you no-good, bug-eyed monster!" Vince shouted. "You just don't blow up my brand-new Humvee and get away with it. You're still under arrest. Turn yourself in, or I'm gonna get nasty!"

If only I had my regular powers, thought Alex, she could get out of her predicament without hurting anyone. But her zapping powers were like her morphing powers, stuck at one weird speed, and she was afraid to use them again. But she had to scare Vince away somehow. Her life depended on it!

Alex hadn't tried her telekinetic abilities yet. When Vince jumped up to take a shot, she concentrated on his weapon and tried to knock it out of his hands. Instead, Vince zoomed straight into the air, and he hovered about twenty feet above them, kicking and shouting. "Put me down!" Vince yelled. "Help! Help!"

His operative, Jackson, jumped to his feet and ran for his life. "Don't vaporize me!" he shrieked.

Alex tried to drop Vince back to earth, but she couldn't make him fall—he was stuck up there. She was willing to leave Vince hanging, but then abruptly, with no effort from her, he dropped to the ground.

Alex couldn't begin to try to understand her

powers at that moment, because a bright search-light suddenly blinded her. It was so bright that Vince—in a heap on the ground—had to cover his eyes. More searchlights slashed through the darkness, and Alex heard the roar of propeller blades chopping the sky.

Helicopters!

She looked up and saw a whole squadron of choppers sweep across the sky, headed straight toward them. Knowing they were looking for her, Alex was terrified. The sound of the slashing blades drove straight to her senses, and her stomach churned in fear.

She scrambled out of the ditch and ran across the cornfield, hoping to hide in a nearby farm-house. But she was so tired after all her efforts that she couldn't get any speed. Feet and legs were good for running, but jellylike flippers were not.

The corn had already been harvested, and the ragged old stalks were only a foot tall. There was nowhere to hide in the field, and the farm-house was too far away. Panting, Alex looked behind her. Two of the helicopters were hov-ering over Vince and his wrecked car. Three more choppers were circling a wide area, and one of them was headed straight for her. Its searchlight cut a bright path across the dark stubbled field.

Alex tripped and sprawled across the dried stumps of corn. She looked up and saw the chopper coming closer, with its powerful searchlight sweeping the ground. It was a military helicopter, probably the National Guard. In another second, it would be on top of her!

From nowhere, a flash of blinding light shot across the sky and hovered directly over Vince's car, looking like a spinning disc of pure light. Alex squinted, awestruck. This was no helicopter—it was a real UFO! Like a blazing nebula, it spun against the darkness, and Alex could only gape at it.

At once, the helicopters swerved away and took off after the UFO. The spaceship rose slowly into the starscape, and the choppers almost caught up with it. But Alex had the feeling that the UFO was toying with them. It could easily lose the choppers, but it wanted them to follow, as if to draw them away from Alex.

Alex didn't have time to think much about her weird savior, because Vince was still out there. Also, the choppers could return any second.

She looked around, wondering exactly where she was. Vince hadn't gotten that far out of town, and she could see city lights in the valley, not far away. That had to be Paradise Valley, and she knew she was on a county road, but she forgot which one.

Shuffling through the dried rows of corn, Alex headed for home, realizing now she was farther away than ever. She glanced over her shoulder and could see the helicopters in the distance. She wondered who—or what—had saved her shiny skin.

Wearing their masks, Annie and Ray walked slowly along the sidewalk. Several people looked at them and grinned or frowned. They didn't pay much attention, because they were trying to follow the mysterious men who had forced their way into Annie's house.

One of them said they had captured an alien, and Annie wanted to see who—or what—this alien was.

The three men were taking an erratic tour through the neighborhood, stopping at some houses but not others. They consulted handheld devices, but Annie couldn't tell what they were doing. At one point, their leader talked into a radio. She wanted to get closer, but she didn't want them to know they were being followed.

So she and Ray mingled with scattered groups of people, blended into the shadows, or hung back as far as they could. It was frustrating, because Annie knew the men could take off any second.

When their quarry stopped at another house, Annie bent down to tie her sneaker. "This isn't working," she muttered. "We can't get close enough. Maybe I should just get the car and try to find my parents."

"Annie," said Ray, peering into the distance. "They're on the move, going fast. One of them is talking on the radio."

Annie bolted to her feet and followed his gaze. She saw the men charge across the street, brushing past everyone. One of them was talking on a portable radio, while the others nervously watched the star-spangled sky. As they swept around a corner house, she and Ray had to hurry to keep up with them. There was no more time to be sneaky or cautious. They could only hope that in their rush, the men weren't paying much attention.

They seem to be headed toward Birch Street, Annie observed, *where all of this started*. It was incredible, but she had only found out about the madness an hour ago. It seemed as if earth had been under siege for days.

Hearing the whoosh of propeller blades, Annie looked up to see a squadron of military helicopters streak across the sky. The noisy choppers were apparently in a hurry to get somewhere, and they made her even more nervous than the police cars.

If this was all a hoax, why was it still going on? Annie wondered. Why were so many people rushing around, acting so paranoid? Who turned the police, the National Guard, and Vince loose on this little town? *Are aliens so bad that we have to make war against them, even if they don't exist?*

Annie couldn't believe that she had thought Mr. Smith was an alien. In this night of craziness, that had to be her most embarrassing moment. *Or maybe it was the present moment*, Annie thought wryly. *I never thought I'd pay good money to wear a little kid's clammy mask.*

The men cut across a corner yard and passed under a streetlamp. Annie and Ray skirted around the side of the house and saw the group tear across the street toward two cargo vans painted white. They kept glancing up into the sky, but they didn't look behind them.

"Come on," Annie whispered.

A moment later, two kids in masks cut across the street and strolled down the sidewalk. Because it was Halloween, nobody paid them much attention. Annie saw the men confer on the street corner; they were looking at a map. She punched Ray's arm and made him walk faster.

They were getting close to the white vans when the meeting between the three men broke up. Two of them jumped in the first vehicle, and the younger one ran toward the second.

The young guy opened the rear door of his vehicle and tossed in some gear. He looked up and saw Ren and Stimpy staring at him. He grinned. "Hey, I love those guys."

Still chuckling, he ran around to the front of his van. Annie noticed that he hadn't locked the rear door, and she inched toward it. When the driver opened his door, she opened the rear. Annie jumped in at the same moment he did, pulling Ray in after her. He grabbed for the door and closed it just as the van roared to life.

Annie tumbled over the gear, and boxes and equipment jabbed her in the back. But she didn't cry out, even when Ray stuck a bony elbow in her knee. The roar of the engine covered their movements as they spilled onto the floor. The vehicle lurched away from the curb, and they were tossed around again. Annie gripped Ray's shirt to make sure she knew where he was. As the road got smoother, they heard some static and a voice on the radio.

"Where are you guys?" It was a voice she didn't recognize. "We need to get out of here!"

"Where's Home Plate?" asked the leader of the van drivers.

"He's chasing the cargo. It got loose. Hey, keep your eyes open—you should see what we've seen tonight! This is a full-scale invasion—UFOs, choppers, I don't know what all. We could be vaporized any second!"

"Ten-four," said the leader. "We should put in for hazardous duty pay. We'll be there in five minutes. Out."

Ray gripped Annie's hand and squeezed nervously.

Feeling like a silver Mylar balloon running out of air, Alex dragged herself across a barren cornfield. She was getting closer to the road, and she didn't know what she would do when she got there. To get back to Paradise Valley, she only knew that she had to cross the road and skirt along beside it. But was she heading back to danger?

She looked nervously behind her, certain that she saw the jagged cornstalks twitching. Somebody was following her, and it had to be Vince. He was the only person in Paradise Valley crazy enough to chase an alien who had just blown up his car.

Alex knew her nemesis well. At that moment, Vince was wearing a T-shirt that was ripped and burned. Much of his shock of blond hair was singed, and there were greasy burns slashed across his face. In his eyes glinted madness and the thrill of the hunt.

Vince lifted his launcher, which was loaded with a second net. "No mealymouthed alien is gonna toss me around and get away with it! This is a fight between you and me. Humankind versus sewer gunk!" He saw a flash on the dark horizon and jogged after it.

Knowing he was bearing down on her, Alex scurried over a ridge, curled into a silver ball, and rolled down into a ditch. When she shook herself off and formed back into a semihuman shape, Alex looked around. She was in a ditch similar to the place where Vince's car was stuck. She had made it back to the road! Thinking about how far she had walked, Alex figured the wreck was about a mile away. And she still had a long way to go.

Because the road was winding and hilly, she couldn't see far in either direction. It looked deserted, but was it safe? One thing was certain, she couldn't stay where she was, not with Vince chasing her. Alex took a deep breath and staggered up the other side of the ditch. She was really getting tired, and every movement felt as if it was draining the life out of her. She could imagine Annie yelling at her, and for once she'd be glad to hear it.

With effort, she dragged herself into the road. At once, she was caught in the glare of headlights—two big vehicles coming fast! The first one honked and began to swerve, and Alex curled into a ball and bounced off the road. Squealing tires just missed hitting her, but she made it to the other side.

"Holy cow!" exclaimed the driver in the second van. "What the heck was that?"

As their van swerved, Annie and Ray bounced around in the back. The driver slammed on the brakes, and they were thrown into a pile. Annie tried not to cry out, even though Ray's foot was on her mouth.

They heard the door creak open, followed by the crunch of the driver's boots in the sand. Annie and Ray took a few seconds to untangle themselves.

"What a ride," Ray moaned.

"Ssshhh!" Annie cautioned. "They're talking."

By holding perfectly still, they could hear every word the men said. "What *was* that thing that streaked across the road?" asked one man.

"It must have been the alien!"

"What are you idiots doing?" asked a breathless, angry voice. Annie recognized it as Vince. "Don't just stand around here doing nothing!"

"Sorry, boss. What should we do?"

"You two, drive that van down the road to the Humvee. Push it, pull it, or drag it—but get my vehicle out of that ditch! You got a towing bar?"

"Okay, but look here, Vince. This mission is more dangerous than we thought. We need more pay."

"I can't believe this!" Vince spat out. "Bloodthirsty aliens are invading the earth, and you're worried about your pay? If we can defeat them and capture one, we'll all be heroes, not to mention filthy rich!'' Vince growled. ''Look at me, all burned and singed! Do I look like I'm having fun?''

''Actually you do.''

''Well, I'm not! Now tow my car away before those choppers come back. Move it!''

When Annie heard the other van start up and drive off, she let out a breath. They were in the van that was staying behind, but what good would it do them?

''Did you see the alien?'' Vince asked the remaining thug.

''Yes, sir.''

''Which way did it go?''

''It slithered off the road right over there, sir.''

''Leave the van here,'' Vince ordered. ''But get a flashlight.''

Annie and Ray ducked down as the driver opened his door to grab a flashlight. Thankfully, he shut the door just as quickly.

''Don't feel sorry for the invader,'' said Vince. ''Nobody invited that *thing* to come to this planet. Remember, it has no respect for our way of life.''

''No, sir.''

''And we have reason to believe there's a

whole colony of them living down in the sewers. Drinking *our* water. Do you want that, soldier?"

"No, sir!"

"Move out!"

Annie heard Vince and the other man scramble down into the ditch. For the moment, she and Ray were alone in the van, parked somewhere on a lonely road.

"Did he leave the keys in the ignition?" asked Ray.

"Let me check." Annie dragged herself to her knees and crawled between the two front seats. Sure enough, their driver had left the keys in the ignition.

"Yes, he left them," she told Ray. "Think I should grab them?"

"They might come in handy," Ray answered. "In fact, you could drive out of here right now, if you wanted."

"No," said Annie. "Vince is chasing some poor creature to death. Even if it's not Alex, we should try to help it. But keep your mask handy, so we won't be recognized."

"Okay," said Ray, staring at the mask of an ugly Chihuahua dog. "I wouldn't want to be without this."

Annie grabbed the car keys and her own mask. "Let's go."

Cautiously, the two of them stepped out of the van into the crisp night air. As far as Annie could tell, they were in the middle of nowhere. She had no idea how they were going to save the hunted alien, but she wasn't going to let Vince capture it.

Looking into the field adjacent to the road, she could see a flashlight beam bobbing in the distance. "That's them," said Annie. "Let's go."

"Remind me to stay home next Halloween," said Ray. He followed her off the road and down into the ditch.

They climbed out of the trench and dashed across the cornfield, chasing the bouncing light.

CHAPTER 10

Alex stumbled and fell. She sat on the ground for several moments, with the stars and hills whirling around her. She could see the lights of Paradise Valley in the distance, but they looked so far away. Between them were hills and forests that stretched forever.

She heard footsteps crunching the ground behind her, and she turned to see the glow of a flashlight. There was nowhere to hide in the barren cornfield, so she had to keep moving.

Dragging herself to her feet, Alex staggered forward. She couldn't run, and she couldn't fight her way out. If Vince didn't get her, maybe she would just collapse out here and eventually dissolve away when it rained. Nobody would ever know what happened to her.

Up one hill and down the other, she pushed herself. She could see lights in one direction and a dark line of trees in the other. They were both so far away that she didn't think she would ever make it. And she was so tired. . . .

"I see it!" came a gleeful shout. "Hurry!"

Alex looked back and could plainly see Vince and one of his henchmen. They were closing fast, running strong and hard. Vince was so close she could see that his teeth were bared. Her only hope left was to scare them away.

She turned around, pointed the silver glob of her index finger at Vince, and tried to zap him. All that came out of her finger was a tiny spark that went about an inch, then fizzled out with a pop. There was no zip in her zap.

"Come on!" Vince shouted excitedly. His instinct for the hunt was well honed after years of practice. He knew from that little spark that his prey was getting weak.

Alex tried to run some more, but she finally collapsed in the field and just lay there, trembling and heaving for breath.

She saw two ominous figures lean over her, and she heard a pop of air. A thick net slammed into her, and she was totally helpless again. This was the end of Alex Mack, the GC-161 kid, and the extraterrestrial. Vince had gotten all three of them with one shot.

He loomed over her, grinning in triumph. "That'll teach you to mess around with humans, you lousy space fungus!"

The other man was younger, and he stared at her with sympathetic eyes. "It looks hurt, or maybe sick," he said.

"Don't get all mushy on me," Vince warned. "If you had seen this thing fry my dashboard, you wouldn't feel sorry for it. Then it tossed me around in the air like a Raggedy Ann doll! And you should see the *mother ship* it came from!" He looked down at Alex and spit on the ground. "It may look innocent, but this thing is nasty."

With his foot, Vince pushed Alex deeper into the thick mesh. She had no energy to resist—she let herself be pushed around like a lump of clay.

"How the worm turns," Vince said with a chuckle. He grabbed the loose ends of the net and started dragging her across the field.

Alex bounced painfully over rocks and clumps of dirt, but she didn't have enough strength left to cry. She thought she would finally pass out.

Halfway across the field, she started wishing she would.

"Unhand that space alien!" a voice shouted.

Vince dropped her on the ground and whirled in the direction of the voice. His hand shaking, the henchman pointed his flashlight toward the voice.

Alex stared as two figures emerged from the darkness. Had they really come to rescue her? She thought she recognized the voice, so she was surprised when she saw who it was.

She had been rescued by . . . Ren and Stimpy?

"I don't know who you jokers are," Vince growled, "but this is *my* prize. You had better beat it, if you know what's good for you."

Their clothes look awfully familiar, Alex thought, staring at the newcomers. *Oh, no.* She realized it was really Annie and Ray! What could they possibly do to stop Vince?

Vince handed the ends of the net to his partner. "Keep dragging it toward the van. I'll take care of these two."

He got down in a karate stance, as if daring them to attack. Then he made a bunch of weird grunts, groans, and karate cries.

"I'm sorry, Mr. Alien, sir," said the young

man as he dragged Alex across the field. "I'm only doing my job."

Ren and Stimpy also did some karate kicks and moves, but they didn't come any closer. Stimpy picked up a rock and threw it at Vince, but he only laughed.

"Is that the best you can do?" he sneered.

Alex felt faint, as if she was going to lose consciousness. But from the corner of her eye, she saw a strange light in the distance. It looked as if it was coming closer.

All of the stars in the sky were dancing, so she didn't know if this light was real or not. It was just the one star that kept getting bigger and bigger. Vince and the others were so busy that they didn't see it. She was the only one paying attention.

Alex remembered the spaceship that had appeared from nowhere to save her before. Was it going to do it again? She was probably just going crazy and imagining things.

At least watching the light kept Alex alert as she was dragged down into the ditch. The van was only a few yards away, and it looked as if nobody could stop Vince. Soon it would be over for the alien formerly known as Alex Mack. She turned back to the weird light and saw it sweep over the hills at a high rate of speed. As it came toward her, the UFO expanded into a huge bank of lights, and the whole sky lit up.

The man dragging her yelled in fright and dropped her on the ground. He scrambled up the hill, trying to get away.

Back in the field, Vince's eyes got as big as flying saucers. "Oh, no! Not them again!" Ignoring the kids in the masks, he ran toward the van. On the way, he grabbed his precious cargo and tried to move it by himself.

A blinding beam of light caught Vince and froze him. Soon all of them were bathed in blinding light, and they dropped to the ground. Alex sat up, because she thought she was going to be rescued.

Until she heard the sound—

Slash, *slash*, *slash!* Five helicopters zoomed toward them as beams of light cut through the darkness. The choppers quickly found the people on the ground and chased them down. Blasts of wind from the whirring propellers almost blew Alex over.

All of them were frozen by the searchlights. If they took a step one way, the lights moved with them. If they stepped the other way, the lights moved with them. There was no escape from the military helicopters that buzzed over the road like a swarm of giant bees.

"All right, everybody freeze where you stand!" ordered a booming voice on a loud-speaker. It took a moment for Alex to realize that the voice was coming from the helicopter over her head. She squinted into the lights and the wind, but couldn't see anything.

"You in the net, hold perfectly still," the voice warned. "You two guys, freeze! Don't get any closer to that van. Everybody hold still—you, too, Ren and Stimpy."

Alex wasn't likely to run anywhere. She was tied up and exhausted. She dreaded to think about what was going to happen next, but at least it wouldn't be at the hands of Vince.

"Run for the van!" came a shout. Vince and his partner made a mad dash to the white van and jumped in before the helicopters could react.

"Give me the keys!" Vince shouted.

"They're in the ignition."

"No, they're not! Give me the keys!" Vince started shaking his henchman.

"Will the two idiots in the van slowly get out," ordered the voice from the helicopter. "I mean it."

The passenger jumped out and flopped on the

ground. Scowling, Vince got out and put his hands up. "Look, we're on your side!" he shouted at the chopper. "I'm an old company man myself!"

"Hold still!" ordered the voice. "We're going to land and take you all into custody."

The helicopter swooped toward Alex, and she thought it would land on top of her. She wanted to tell them that the kids in the costumes were innocent. It was all a prank, an innocent joke! But it didn't seem that way anymore.

Suddenly another light appeared on the dark horizon. *Just what we need,* thought Alex, *more helicopters. Everyone should join the party!* Maybe they would all get their pictures in the newspaper—the heroes who captured the dangerous alien.

This new light zoomed toward them at a really amazing rate of speed. *This has to be the super-duper helicopter,* Alex thought. She almost closed her eyes, because she couldn't stand to see any more people chasing her.

In front of her, the helicopter stopped its landing. In fact, it lifted into the sky and began to circle as if it was afraid. All of the choppers flew high into the air and began to buzz around like angry hornets.

From far off, the amazing light got closer. It never turned into a squadron of helicopters as Alex expected. It never turned into anything—it just washed over them like a soothing breeze. Alex's aching body seemed to relax, and all the pain and tension mysteriously drained from her.

Even Vince wore a warm, fuzzy smile as he stared into the intense light. Alex forgot what she was worried about, and everything seemed fine.

"Alex!" said a familiar voice. She felt a hand shaking her shoulder. "Alex! Wake up, honey."

Alex stirred awake and looked around the darkened bedroom she shared with her sister. Gee, what a terrible dream she'd been having— she would have to tell Annie about it. Yes, there was Annie, asleep in her own bed.

"Wake up!" said the voice urgently. She knew it was her father.

"Come on, Dad," she muttered. "It's not time for school yet. It's still dark out."

"That's because it's night," George said. "Halloween night! Where have you been? We've been looking all over for you."

Alex suddenly realized that she was wearing her miniskirt, sparkly top, and alien costume.

She was in bed with all her clothes on, and her bedroom was full of people.

Standing in front of her were her mom and dad, and Nicole and Robyn. Ray walked in yawning, and he looked just as puzzled as she felt. Annie was also lying in bed with all her clothes on, and she sat up in surprise.

It wasn't often that Annie looked totally confused, but this was one of those magic moments. She blinked at Alex and yawned. "What happened?"

"That's what we're trying to figure out," Mrs. Mack said. "We came home and found Ray asleep on the couch downstairs. We asked him where you were, and he said he didn't know. Then we came up here and found you asleep in your beds."

"Uh, yeah," said Alex, trying to think. Bits and pieces of her memory were coming back to her, but not enough to tell anyone. She doubted if she was thinking clearly enough to even make up a good story.

Suddenly there was a knock on the door frame, and everyone turned to look. The mysterious Mr. Jonathan Smith was standing in the doorway.

"Excuse me, the door was open, and I heard

voices." He took one look at Alex and smiled. "Oh, good, the young ladies are in bed."

"Do you know something about that?" George asked.

"Yes, I do," Mr. Smith answered. "I saw them walking around, looking dazed, and I brought them home. The police said someone was squirting pepper gas into the crowd."

"Oh, no!" Barbara Mack gasped.

"Yes, it confuses people. They become disoriented." He gazed at Alex. "Do you remember now, me finding you and bringing you home?"

She nodded quickly. "Yes, yes!" That wasn't what she remembered, but what she remembered couldn't possibly have happened. *Or did it?* Anyway, she wasn't going to tell her parents about it.

Gratefully, her dad shook Mr. Smith's hand. "Thank you so much for bringing them home. I can't believe what a crazy Halloween this has been. Did you hear about the alien invasion?"

"Yes," said the stranger, shaking his head. "A few lights in the sky and a bad joke on the radio, and you've got an invasion. The tricks were especially bad this Halloween."

"Yes, they were," said George, looking pointedly at Alex. "And my daughter was involved with that one."

If you only knew, Alex thought.

Mr. Smith tipped his hat. "I have to be going now. There are several people to whom I must say good-bye. It's been a pleasure being your neighbor, Mr. Mack. Your family is quite special." He winked at Alex.

Everybody said good-bye to the stranger, and he slipped quietly out the door.

"All right," said Barbara, "we've had enough excitement for one night. I think everybody should go home and get into their own beds."

"Good night, Alex," said Robyn. "I'm glad to see you weren't abducted by aliens. But where did you go?"

"I'll talk to you guys tomorrow," Alex promised. *After I figure out what to tell you*, she added silently.

"Good night," said Ray, still scratching his head and looking puzzled.

"Good night," said Alex.

When everybody was gone, Alex stood up and walked into the bathroom. She thought she would have to take off her green makeup and purple hair tint. But when she looked in the mirror, her face and hair were already clean!

She walked out of the bathroom and sat on the end of Annie's bed. Her sister was looking at a squashed piece of plastic. "What is that?" asked Alex.

"It's a Stimpy mask," Annie said, turning the goofy mask around for Alex to look at.

"I knew that was you. Thanks for trying to save me."

Annie rubbed her eyes. "Thank Mr. Smith. He pulled it off—somehow."

Alex stood and walked to her window. She gazed upon the twinkling stars in the black soup of space. What did all of it mean? Was there anything out there, or just their own fears, hopes, and imaginations?

Well, Alex thought, *my alien costume sure was a big success*. She saw a bright meteorite streaking across the sky and made a wish. No more sci-fi Halloweens.

CHAPTER 11

The next morning, Alex awoke with a mild headache. Otherwise, she was okay after the ordeal of Halloween. Parts of the night were still too dreamlike to believe, but she remembered that Mr. Smith had brought her home.

When she went down to breakfast, her dad was hogging the newspaper as usual. Both Annie and her mom were trying to snatch it away from him, but he held on to the front page.

"Come on, George, at least read the articles out loud," said Barbara.

"Okay," George agreed. He looked up and saw Alex enter the kitchen. "Hi, sweetheart, have a seat."

"Thanks, Dad." Alex slipped into her customary chair at the table.

"How do you feel?"

"Fine."

"What's in the newspaper?" Annie demanded, still looking troubled about the night before.

"There are several articles related to last night," said George. "Here, this is the main one." He showed them the headline, which read: Halloween Invaders Stalk Paradise Valley.

George read aloud, " 'Reports of UFOs and extraterrestrials caused a panic in the streets of Paradise Valley last night. The sightings began two days earlier but climaxed while children were trick-or-treating on Halloween.

" 'Despite hundreds of calls to news outlets, police were quick to claim the alien sightings were a hoax. They point to the confession of Louis Driscoll, the student deejay at the high school radio station.

" 'According to Driscoll, at his urging, several of his friends called the station to report alien sightings. The hoax was an attempt to mimic Orson Welles's 1938 broadcast of *War of the Worlds*.

" 'Sergeant Theresa Washburn of the Paradise Valley Police Department told reporters, "The story snowballed and people panicked. Mobs were roaming the streets, breaking into homes and backyards. But no aliens were found. It was a case of mass hysteria." ' "

George glanced at Annie. "Just like you said, sweetie." But Annie still looked unconvinced.

He kept reading: " 'This explanation has not satisfied many residents of Paradise Valley, who claim to have seen the aliens. "It was a big shiny thing," said Wilbur Mitchell of Elm Street. "And it attacked my dog." ' "

"Liar," Alex muttered.

"Pardon me?" George asked.

"Never mind." Alex smiled sweetly. "Go on."

George continued: " 'Despite the number of people who reported seeing aliens, no physical evidence was found to support the claims. Police continue to treat the matter as a hoax that got out of hand.' "

"What about the helicopters?" Barbara asked.

"I'm getting to that," said George. " 'Sent to investigate, National Guard helicopters reported seeing weather balloons and other natural phenomena. Said Captain Williams of the Guard, "There have been a large number of meteor showers in the sky the last few nights. This might also have alarmed people and caused some of these reports." ' "

Annie looked at Alex, who knew what her sister was thinking. The people in the helicopters had seen more than meteor showers, but they didn't get their hands on anything. They had no proof of what they saw, so they denied seeing it. In a way, she didn't blame them, because she and Annie were doing the same thing.

George read some more. " 'No one has filed a claim of missing persons, and nothing has been stolen, except for a bedsheet reported missing on Adams Avenue.' "

Alex snorted in surprise, and she quickly took a drink of milk.

"The article goes on," said George, "with more comments from people who thought they saw UFOs. I can't believe how silly people can be."

"Isn't it true?" said Annie with a nervous laugh. "What is that article down in the corner? The one about the zoo?"

George frowned as he read it. "Oh, this story is about Vince. Boy, has he sunk low since he got fired from the plant. They found him asleep last night in the baboon cage at the zoo. He claimed aliens abducted him and put him there.

The police took him away for psychological evaluation.

"Oh, yes," said George, "Louis will have to pay a fine for creating a public nuisance."

"Every cloud has a silver lining," said Alex. She was beginning to feel better.

George found something else. "Oh, and here's an article about the pepper spray incident on Waverly."

Annie glance at Alex and said, "Oh, it really happened."

"Of course it really happened," said George. "How did you girls get all the way up there?"

Alex shrugged. "You know how it is, Dad. You do a lot of walking on Halloween."

"You sure do," Annie agreed.

George tossed the newspaper on the table and stood up. "Well, I'm off to work. There should be plenty of things to talk about around the water cooler today."

Barbara gave him a peck on the cheek. "Have a good day, honey."

"You, too. Bye, girls!" They said good-bye to their father, and he headed to the garage.

A few minutes later, their mom left for school and Alex and Annie were alone at the dining-room table.

"I almost lost it last night," Alex admitted.

"I know," said Annie. "You've got to be careful—all that makeup and hair tint must have upset your chemical balance. Other kids can do stuff like that, but not you. You've got to watch your electrolytes."

Alex stared into the distance. "I wonder how we got home last night."

"I don't want to know," said Annie. She picked up their breakfast dishes and took them to the sink.

Alex picked up a towel and helped her dry the dishes. "One thing I do know is that you and Ray were crazy to come after me. But I really love you because of it."

They hugged, and Annie smiled. "Hey, you're the only sister I've got."

"And to prove how thankful I am," said Alex, "I'm going to do you a big favor."

"Oh, yeah. What?"

"Next Halloween, I'm going to wear my regular clothes and stay home and hand out candy. *You* can go out on Halloween for a change."

"No way!" Annie exclaimed, horrified. "That's *my* job. I do the candy. You wouldn't even know what to buy."

"Oh, sure I would. About *twice* as much as you buy."

"That's wasteful," said Annie. "As the oldest, I get to stay home on Halloween—"

"Says who?"

The good-natured bickering of the two earthling sisters could be heard out in the yard as a cool autumn day dawned on Paradise Valley.

About the Author

John Vornholt lives in Tucson, Arizona, with his wife, Nancy, and two children, Sarah and Eric. He used to live in Los Angeles and write TV shows, but he's been writing books since 1989. During that time, he's written almost thirty of them, including three *Starfleet Academy* stories, two *Dinotopia* stories, five *Warrior of Virtue* books, a bunch of *Star Trek* novels, and works such as *The Fabulist* and *How to Sneak into the Girls' Locker Room*. John has also written an *Are You Afraid of the Dark?* book entitled *The Tale of the Ghost Riders*.

Before he became a writer full-time, he was a stunt man and actor, and worked in the computer and tourist businesses. John always advises would-be writers to "Do interesting things with your life; then you'll have something to write about."

Sometimes, it takes a kid to solve a good crime....

Original stories based on the hit Nickelodeon show!

#1 A Slash in the Night
by Alan Goodman

#2 Takeout Stakeout
By Diana G. Gallagher

#3 Hot Rock
by John Peel

#4 Rock 'n' Roll Robbery
by Lydia C. Marano and David Cody Weiss

(Coming in mid-October 1997)

To find out more about *The Mystery Files of Shelby Woo* or any other Nickelodeon show, visit Nickelodeon Online on America Online (Keyword: NICK) or send e-mail (NickMailDD@aol.com).

A MINSTREL BOOK
Published by Pocket Books

1338-02

Have you ever wished for the complete guide to surviving your teenage years? At long last, here's your owner's manual—a book of instructions and insights into exactly how YOU operate.

LET'S TALK ABOUT ME!

A Girl's Personal, Private, and Portable Instruction Book for life

Learn what makes boys so weird
Discover the hidden meanings in your doodles
Uncover the person you want to be
Get to know yourself better than anyone else on Earth
Laugh a little
Think a little
Grow a little

TOP-SECRET QUIZZES, COOL ACTIVITIES, AND MUCH, MUCH MORE

Being a teenage girl
has never been so much fun!

**From the creators of
the bestselling CD-ROM!**

An Archway Paperback
Published by Pocket Books

1384-01